*Pride Publishing books by Xenia Melzer*

**Demon Mates**
Demon's Wish
Demon's Game
Demon's Dance

I0670564

# Demon Mates

# DEMON'S DANCE

# XENIA MELZER

Demon's Dance
ISBN # 978-1-80250-999-1
©Copyright Xenia Melzer 2022
Cover Art by Erin Dameron-Hill ©Copyright November 2022
Interior text design by Claire Siemaszkiewicz
Pride Publishing

Published in 2022 by Pride Publishing, United Kingdom.

Pride Publishing is an imprint of Totally Entwined Group Limited.

# DEMON'S DANCE

# Dedication

To Steffi, our dancing instructor. I love your
patented 'That wasn't too bad, but...'
For my daughters. Herding you is easier than
looking after demons. Still, you give me the best
ideas.

# Acknowledgements

I have to thank AJ Sherwood for the idea with the renaissance fair. In her book *The Tribulations of Ross Young, Supernat PA*, she let her paranormals take part in a LARP event. It made such an impression on me that when I worked on *Demon's Dance*, the scene with the renaissance fair almost wrote itself. Thank you, AJ, for this wonderful writing prompt!

# Chapter One

Alerion, King of all Demons, the Mighty Warrior, Defeater of the Unruly, was flat on his back somewhere in a clearing in Canada, trying to comprehend what had just happened. There had been two growls, the nuance less threatening and more possessive, then a dual *"Ours"*, followed by two muscular bodies barreling into him. As he had just been talking to his favorite son Sammy — although he had a feeling Jon would soon join Sammy on that pedestal — the attack had taken him by surprise.

It was hard to hear anything over the excessive sniffing taking place on both sides of his neck, but from what he could discern, people were rather more amused than worried. From somewhere, a *"Well, fuck me sideways!"* drifted to his ears, of no real consequence because the scent enveloping him — raspberries and cream with an undertone of cinnamon and clove — was way too pleasant to be thinking about anything else.

The declarations of *"Mate!"*, *"Ours!"* and *"Claim!"* left him in no doubt as to what was happening.

*I'm so lucky my mates are shifters!* Otherwise, it would be the same back and forth that his sons Dre and Barion had had with their mates, and Alerion knew he could do without that drama in his life. In fact, ruling all demonkind was a drama in and of itself, which was why he tried to avoid it in all other aspects of his life — not that there was so much going on aside from cowing unruly demons and patiently explaining for the three-millionth time how nobody was as sturdy as a demon and, therefore, playing with other species — humans in particular — was forbidden. Nobody could accuse demons of being quick on the uptake.

"Uhm, Declan? Troy? Could you perhaps let Dad up?" Of course it was Sammy, the best son-in-law a demon king could wish for, who tried to end the spectacle. Alerion was of two minds about the sniffing ending because yes, getting to see his mates would be nice, no doubt, but on the other hand, it was also *very* nice to be so close to them.

"I'm not sure they can hear you, Sammy dear." *One of the witches...Mavis or Maribell.* Alerion didn't know them well enough to identify them by voice alone.

"Why do I have the sudden urge to bare my neck?" Jon, on the other hand, was easy to pick out.

"You're not baring your neck to anybody but me." *Barion, growling like a lion defending a fresh kill.*

"I didn't say I would do it — just that I have the feeling I should." Jon sounded part wounded, part soothing.

"What are we baring and why? Is this some custom nobody has told me about?" *Amber, the banshee,* Alerion thought. Her voice was quite distinctive, the screech to warn heroes of their impending death always present as an undertone. Most people couldn't discern it and just found Banshees' voices a bit unnerving, but Alerion wasn't most people.

"Well, I'm always up for a little baring of body parts." That voice sounded adventurous. It had to be Corrywin's mate, Jon's Grann, the Voodoo priestess. Interesting woman and a perfect fit for his restless uncle.

"As much as I love all your body parts, *ma chere*, I think we should be helping Alerion first." *Corrywin, helpful as always...not.*

"I thought we had to get naked?" Amber again.

"Nobody is baring anything!" Dre, his second oldest son, the lucky bastard who'd snatched Sammy.

"Can somebody explain to me what's going on?" Judging from the harmonious sound, it had to be Emilia, the vampire. Alerion liked her because she was very down-to-earth, despite her royal ancestry.

"It's simple, dear," one of the witches said. "Declan and Troy have finally found their third, and in their exuberance, they have forgotten not only their manners but also to shield their auras, which can be overwhelming, since they are uber alphas—hence the urge to show submission. Declan! Troy! Stop with the sniffing and get up. Your mate must be uncomfortable with both of you pinning him down."

The last sentences were said with a scolding undertone of 'bad boys!', which caused the sniffing to stop. Alerion bemoaned this for about half a second before he realized he was now free to admire his mates.

"What's an uber alpha?" Sammy again, always eager to learn. What a smart son he had gained!

Once more, it was one of the witches answering. "Uber alphas are very rare. The last one was born some two hundred and fifty years ago. They are so powerful all shifters immediately unite under them, which inevitably leads to bloody war. One prime example is Napoleon Bonaparte, the French emperor. He was the last uber alpha we knew of until Declan and Troy came along."

"Wow. Are you planning to do that any time soon? It's just that war is such a waste of lives and time." Sammy was addressing Alerion's mates, who had lifted their heads enough to stare at Sammy, which in turn gave Alerion a wonderful view of their breathtaking profiles. One of them was blond, the other's hair a rich dark brown. Their noses were sharp, their jaws like carved marble and their skin flawless perfection.

"Sammy, we're having a moment here!" the blond whined, his hands still resting on Alerion's chest, which he didn't mind at all.

"I can see that, Declan, but you have to admit that impending war is kind of a serious topic."

So, his blond mate was Declan — which meant the dark-haired one had to be Troy, who was the next to speak. "Sammy, how long do you know us? Three years? Four? Have you ever gotten the impression we would strive for world domination?"

Through the space between his mates' faces, Alerion could see Sammy furrowing his brows. *My son is a such a thinker! And my mates are so gorgeous!*

"Well, you're certainly rich enough to buy large parts of it," Emilia said matter-of-factly.

"Says the vampire with the *very* old money," Amber said, winking.

"So you don't want to wage bloody war?" Sammy sounded so happy.

"No." Declan sighed. "We don't like messes, remember?"

"Uh, almost forgot that. Well, a battlefield certainly isn't the place for somebody who dusts the *undersides* of their windowsills." Emilia grinned. "A trait I deeply admire."

"Because you completely lack it?" Troy raised the brow Alerion could see from his place on the ground. It almost made him swoon. *So beautiful.*

"I guess a battlefield is kind of messy—and unsanitary." Jon seemed to be deep in thought.

"If you wanted to conquer the world, you would tell us, wouldn't you?" Amber sounded suspicious.

"Nobody is conquering anything—or waging bloody war or buying the world! All Declan and I want is to get our mate somewhere quiet with a nice big bed—emphasis on quiet. If you would excuse us?" Troy gracefully got up, offering Alerion his hand. Declan was on his feet as well, staring at Alerion as if he were a bloody steak and Declan was starved. It was nice to be looked at with such hunger. Alerion felt his cock, which had been hard since the moment his mates had tackled him to the ground, twitching.

"Yes, I think a quiet place would be nice. How about we visit my little cabin in Whitewater where we can...proceed." Alerion had tried for subtlety and obviously failed spectacularly, given how everybody gathered around them was snickering. The two witches, Mavis and Maribell, seemed to have their own little film going on in their heads while Grann was shamelessly making out with Corrywin. Sammy stared at them with big eyes — he was still so innocent, bless his sweetness — while Jon smiled at them encouragingly.

"Yes, let's proceed." Troy winked.

Both alphas were still holding Alerion's hands, and he tried to decide which one he should let go of to slice space and time when Dre stepped forward with a long-suffering sigh and solved this terrible conundrum by doing the slicing for him — he, too, was a good son and had brought Sammy into the family after all — and nodded at him. "Have fun, Dad. And congratulations. Declan, Troy, congratulations to you as well. If you hurt my dad —"

"Yeah, yeah, you will do to us what we will do to you and Barion if you hurt Sammy or Jon." Declan was already stepping toward the slice.

"I just wanted to have it out in the open."

"It is. Bye. Enjoy the party." Troy was following his mate, tugging Alerion along. He knew his smile had to be showing all his teeth, but he was on his way to mate with the two most gorgeous creatures that had ever lived!

"Dre, thank you. Barion, Jon, I'm sorry I'm leaving so soon. I'm going to invite you to dinner. Promise. Sammy, don't worry."

They all waved, Jon saying something along the lines of "Finding your mate is the most important thing!" while Sammy was furiously wiping away his tears and simultaneously smiling so hard that his cheeks had to hurt.

"Congratulations, Dad, and have fun! You too, Declan, Troy."

"See you next Wednesday!"

Alerion stepped into the slice in space still holding the hands of both his mates. This day was certainly one to be remembered.

# Chapter Two

As it turned out, Dre had opened the slice in time and space directly into a spacious bedroom. While Declan took in the huge room with the gigantic four-poster facing a window wall that gave a breathtaking view over the mountains of Whitewater, he realized that 'cabin' was not an accurate word to describe Alerion's home. Words like 'mansion' or even 'small palace' came to mind.

It wasn't important, anyway. They had found their third—a bit of a surprise, because they hadn't thought they would get one, despite, or rather because of what the Shifter Council had told them, bunch of boring old farts they were—and the claiming was imminent. Alerion was very much not an omega, which amused Declan to no end, because he could already picture the faces of the council members once they found out there wasn't a meek little birthing machine bound to them, but one of the most alpha types ever. Fate, it seemed, had a *great* sense of humor.

Declan's cock twitched in his pants, effectively dragging him back to reality. It was, he decided, because both his mates smelled so divine. He was used to the spicy tones of Troy's arousal, after all. They had sex at least once a day. Werewolf stamina was a thing of beauty. Alerion's scent was more subtle, softer, a caress of lavender and chocolate. All their scents combined were a potent drug that made it hard to think—and thinking was important. He knew that much. He just couldn't remember why.

"Uhm, before we get rid of our clothes, let's have a brief chat." Alerion's voice sounded strained, his eyes glowing red. Yeah, not much thinking going with him, either—or not for long.

"About what?" Troy's fangs were already half out, his shirt ripping at the seams.

"The logistics, I guess. I assume that you two are already mated, but I can't see your mating scars." Alerion didn't sound too surprised. As old as he was, he probably knew a lot more than they did. Declan managed to clear the lusty fog from his brain long enough to form a coherent answer.

"Yes, we have claimed each other. Scars didn't take, but we have the bond." He didn't want to go into detail as to why the scars hadn't taken. For one, they didn't really know. It was all speculation, but the most likely scenario, as suggested by Mavis and Maribel, was that without their third, the bond wasn't complete and therefore the scars didn't show. Now that they had indeed found their missing mate, the scars should become visible as soon as the bond was completed. And if not, biting Troy again was no hardship.

"Ah, I see." Alerion nodded. He really seemed to know something, which wasn't important at the moment. Important was to get naked and their cocks and teeth into their mate.

"How do you want to do this?" Alerion couldn't be serious. It was sex. Not overly complicated, even if there were three people involved.

"For our bite to take, we need to fuck you," Troy said, seemingly at the very edge of his self-restraint.

Alerion remained silent, and for a long moment, Declan was afraid their mate was one of those stuck-up dominant males who didn't bottom, which would be a problem—a huge one, bigger than the bed they still weren't rolling around in.

"If you don't like us to top you—" he started.

Alerion waved him off.

"I love bottoming. Every kind of sex, actually. No, I'm more concerned about my bite. Once I get my teeth in you, there will be pain, which means an end to the fun times for several hours, at least. I hate to say it, but we'll have to do this in stages."

"Don't care." Troy was ripping off his shirt with one clawed hand, while tugging at his trousers with the other. The poor fabric stood no chance. "Want you now. *Need* you."

Exactly Declan's sentiment. He started to follow Troy's shining example and get naked. Almost absently, Alerion did the same. Declan had known the sound of ripping fabric was erotic as hell but this— hearing it and getting the visual of both his mates baring their gorgeous bodies... Troy's body was bulging with muscle, and Alerion's did as well, but with skin already morphing into scales, beautiful black scales Declan wanted to lick. He knew from Sammy that despite being able to withstand any mortal blade, the scales felt smooth and silky to the touch. He and

Troy had been miffed when both Dre and Barion had refused to let them cop a feel, but now they had their very own demon to touch as much as they pleased.

"I'd say for the first round, you get to fuck and claim me while Troy fucks and claims you. Once I'm in working order again, we switch. Plan?" That was what Declan had intended to say. Somehow, on the way from his brain to his tongue, the sentence turned into, "You fuck me, Troy you," accompanied by guttural grunts Declan couldn't believe he was capable of. His men seemed to understand him perfectly, though, because Troy was already pushing him onto the bed, dragging Alerion along. Declan landed on his back, had a split second to admire the perfect softness of the mattress, and was then bracketed by Alerion's broad frame. His mate was mighty fine, half shifted into his demon form, his black scales with the golden tattoos so gorgeous that they took Declan's breath away. His equally black hair had transformed into shimmering scales running down his back, which Declan could see clearly in the mirror on the ceiling of the four-poster. What an ingenious idea to have one there. Declan could not only see his new mate but also Troy, who was getting into position behind Alerion, draping his muscled body over their demon's back.

"Sorry. Can't go slow," Alerion growled, grabbing Declan's knees and hoisting his legs onto his shoulders.

Declan felt a cool breeze down there, quickly followed by the heat radiating from Alerion's skin as he gently stroked Declan's hole with his fingers. They were huge, holding the promise of a good pounding that Declan would feel for days, despite his werewolf healing. He couldn't wait.

"Lube," Troy rumbled from behind Alerion, his fingers as busy as those of the demon as Declan could see in the mirror. Oh, the games they would be playing once the urgency of the claiming was out of the way!

"Bedside," Alerion panted.

Troy swore because he couldn't reach the nightstand without letting go of Alerion. Declan could relate. He wouldn't want to let go of their mate, either. And luckily, he didn't have to. Being the bottom bread in their sandwich had its perks. Troy used his werewolf speed to get the lube, squeezed it enthusiastically over Alerion's crack, likely making the scales gleam in the sunlight that came in through the windows. Troy then handed the lube to Alerion, who got a generous amount on Declan's balls, smearing it along his taint from there, until he reached his hole. The fingers were as glorious as Declan had known they would be. Through the mate bond, he could feel Troy's excitement at preparing their mate for his cock, which bled into his own about being prepared for Alerion. It was a heady mixture, dragging him under fast.

Troy and Alerion had found a rhythm, their movements in perfect sync. Declan let himself sink into it, enjoying the show and the sensations alike.

After what felt like a torturous eternity, Alerion retracted his fingers, gathered some more lube from the crease between Declan's balls and thighs, and slicked up his own cock. In the mirror, Declan saw Troy getting ready as well, then Alerion's glorious cock nudged Declan's entrance before he sank slowly into him, taking his breath away. Despite everything being almost too much—having found their third, having both his mates in the same bed, being ridden hard by his wolf's instincts to *claim, claim, claim,* while his synapses went crazy from the glorious aroma of the three of them—he could still distinctly feel his entire body singing in happy anticipation, joining the exultation coming from Troy. Being taken and taking was perfect. Both Alerion and Troy set a quick pace from the beginning, the urge to claim and bond too powerful to tame.

When they reached their peaks, Alerion bent forward and Declan exposed his neck, inviting his demon to give him his bite. Troy followed Alerion, sinking his fangs into the junction between Alerion's neck and shoulder only a moment before Declan felt Alerion's fangs pierce his skin. He wouldn't have been able to suppress the howl of pleasure if his life had depended on it—which it didn't, thankfully. His orgasm swept over him with a force he had experienced only once before—when he and Troy had claimed each other.

His demon mate's poison was pumped into his bloodstream, and Declan could feel it, a slight burn and sting but not even remotely as bad as Sammy and Jon had made it sound, which couldn't be right. He had always suspected the two had exaggerated when it came to the pain when their DNA had taken on some demonic characteristics—or it was because Sammy was human and Jon a zombie? Werewolves were probably superior, and their enhanced healing dealt with the poison much quicker than a normal body could. *Or,* Declan thought when he caught sight of Alerion's frown. *Something is wrong.*

There had to be, otherwise Alerion wouldn't look like a confused puppy whose favorite toy had been hidden from sight. Declan felt the ecstasy of his orgasm subsiding almost quicker than it had come.

"Why am I not writhing in pain?"

Alerion backed up a bit, giving Declan a glorious view of his broad chest. A seemingly endless expanse of glimmering scales over hard muscle that he so wanted to touch—but he really should be paying attention to the problem at hand. Troy had his hands on Alerion's shoulders, peeking over his left side with worry in his eyes. "What's wrong?"

Alerion extended a hand, lightly touching Declan's bite wound. He frowned a bit more, then he started grinning. It was as if the sun was coming out after a heavy storm. "Everything is fine. The process has started, but it's missing a piece. It makes sense since you two are already claimed. The magic probably sees you as a unit." He turned his head to Troy. "Quick, change places with Declan."

Declan felt his cock harden so fast that it slapped against his belly. Shifter stamina, especially during a claiming, was a wonderful thing. He hurried to roll aside, making room for Troy, who assumed his position under Alerion with lightning speed while Declan was treated to the stunning sight of their mate's back and ass.

And what a glorious ass it was. He put his hands on the hard cheeks, watching in awe as scales rippled over the skin, enticing him to come closer. He kissed each globe, almost laughing when the scales tickled his lips. Through their bond, Declan could feel Troy's rising lust while Alerion prepared him for the next round of their claiming. Declan turned his attention to Alerion's hole, which was winking at him, the rim slightly puffy and glistening from lube and Troy's essence alike. Knowing how delicious his alpha mate tasted, Declan bent down to do a quick sweep with his tongue, relishing the moans he got from both Alerion and Troy. He licked some more, for the fun of it, tuning in to Troy so he would know when he could enter Alerion. After another eternity — which in reality couldn't have been more than a few minutes, but reality was *so* overrated anyway — Alerion finally slipped his fingers from Troy's hole, only to align his cock immediately.

Declan stopped eating the demon's hole and hurried to get some lube on his own shaft. He managed to slide into Alerion the same moment Alerion entered Troy. Again, the double whammy of penetrating and getting Troy's feeling of being penetrated through their bond pushed him to the edge faster than light traveled. Their rhythm was even quicker and more desperate this time around, Troy howling in pleasure, Alerion grunting with each thrust he gave and received. Declan knew he was making sounds as well.

Their mutual orgasm approached fast, attacking them like a vicious wolverine up front. Alerion surged forward, Troy's exposed neck his goal. Declan followed, but had the presence of mind to veer right, knowing Troy had bitten their demon on the left. When he sank his fangs into Alerion's skin, it was like standing under an ice-cold shower while being thrown into a volcano. His body didn't know what to do with all the different sensations rushing through it and was close to shutting down.

Which was the moment the pain set in. Declan couldn't say he'd been looking forward to it, but a part of him was relieved. After all the drama surrounding Sammy's joining with Dre, he wanted his own mating with a demon to go as smoothly as possible. The lack of a reaction after Alerion had bitten him had worried him more than he'd wanted to admit, and thankfully his brain had been flooded with sex hormones or his fretting would have ruined the second part of their claiming. So, yes, the pain was not exactly welcome, because it hurt like a fucking bitch, but it put Declan's worries to an effective rest.

# Chapter Three

Troy looked around for Declan. He knew they both had blacked out from the pain caused by Alerion's poison running through their veins, changing them into the mates of a demon. There was a groan, and he found Declan leaning on a silvery rock. They were in some kind of mountain landscape, with a Nordic-looking forest in the distance and a lot of stones around them.

"Are you all right?" He helped Declan to get upright.

"Yeah. Just... Well, I guess I have to apologize to Sammy and Jon. I thought they were exaggerating about the pain."

"We both did." Troy scanned the area around them with all his senses. He was pretty sure they weren't alone. "I'm just wondering who we're going to meet. Our parents are still alive, not that we'd want to meet them, and Papa Legba has no business with us," he said the last bit a little louder than necessary.

"That mangy snack had better not," a rumbling voice sounded from behind another boulder a little higher up on the slope they were standing on.

Troy grinned. He might not have been able to detect the other creature with any of his senses, but his instincts were obviously working overtime. Something moved behind the boulder, then the biggest wolf Troy had ever seen stepped forward.

"Fenris." Declan sounded more annoyed than awed, a sentiment Troy shared. The first werewolf ever had visited them in their dreams the night before they were supposed to fight each other to the death. His speech to both of them had been the same — yeah, you could be of godly descent and still as unimaginative as a stone — and not helped endear him to them. It was all the talk about 'killing and maiming and drenching the whole world in blood in addition to the ruling over it' that had upset both of them.

In Troy's opinion, Fenris was a true relic of a past, where things admittedly had been easier but also a lot less pleasant and sanitary than now, who hadn't managed to adapt to the changing world. Now, he was a snarling reminder of why change was not always bad and, in his case, desperately needed, watching from the outside without any true influence left and angry because of it — not the most pleasant combination when the creature in question was the child of a trickster god destined to destroy the world. It made most other gods look positively endearing in comparison — not that Troy had met any. Still...he didn't think it could be *worse*.

"What do you want this time?" Troy had neither reason nor the will to be friendly. This mangy fleabag had tried to make him kill Declan. Next to him, Declan put a hand on his lower back, silently assuring him of his love and support. *Oh, the joys of having a mate!*

"Nothing." Troy hadn't thought it possible, but the mighty predator looked petulant. His teeth were bared, as usual. Troy had a suspicion that Fenris couldn't get his chops down far enough to cover them, a case for a vet if ever there was one, but he wouldn't mention it, because as much as he wanted to aggravate his supposed god, he did not have a death wish, not when he had just found his third.

"If you want nothing, then why are we here?" The suspicion in Declan's tone mirrored Troy's own.

"Don't ask me. Probably to rub it in." Fenris's voice came out as an angry snarl. Angry was in his factory settings, so no surprise there.

"Huh? To rub *what* in?" Troy glanced at Declan who shrugged.

"Don't play dumber than you are. How my plans have been foiled by the fates!" Fenris roared so loud, a few pebbles on the slope started sliding down. His enraged howl echoed through the mountain landscape, making Troy a bit nervous. The last thing he wanted was to have front row seats for a rockslide.

"You two were supposed to rule this world! To bathe it in blood! Well, one of you—the one who survived the fight. At least I hoped one of you would survive it. You wouldn't believe how many uber alphas have managed to kill each other before any ruling could take place. But there have to be two, because of competition. It makes a wolf stronger, keeps them on their toes, and a bit of friendly fighting to determine who's boss has never hurt anybody—not in my time, at least. We were all about the fight, not like folks today—giving out *participation awards*, for Odin's sake. What's that supposed to be? 'Thank you for being there, even though you're as useful as a three-legged wolf on a hunt? And nobody will ever want to mate with you, not with those genes. And what makes you think taking part is a good idea when you're clearly better off petting some snails, but only the sick ones, because a normal one would be too dangerous for you?'" The wolf shook his head, shaking the fur around his neck, which always looked wet, reminding Troy more of a muskrat than a dangerous predator. "Where was I?" Fenris also tended to lose his train of thought when he got into one of his rants. So basically, he was just rambling all the time, never really coming to the point.

"Bathing the world in blood," Declan supplied helpfully. Troy could feel that his mate wanted to get it over with so they could return to their demon.

"Ah, yes. At least you're listening. You should have made the werewolves mighty again—made them the ruling species, as it was meant to be. I had such a good prophesy, too. Sent it to a proper *Völva*, the most powerful around. *The chosen ones shall fight for the crown of the world, and the winner shall reign over all of Earth, the greatest empire there ever was.* I didn't even go for subtlety or double meaning this time. No, just a straight declaration of what should come to pass. And what happened instead? Look at you! Mated to each other! Two alphas! Uber-alphas at that. What a joke."

Troy shared a look with Declan. They were both waiting for foam to appear around Fenris's jaws. He had clearly left sane far behind and was speeding through batshit crazy, destination a *Cthulu* kind of madness.

"Uhm, last time we checked, fated mates trumped everything, even the most straightforward prophesies. We do rule a great portion of the financial world, though." At this point, Troy wasn't sure if he wanted to soothe the beast—he did look a bit pitiful, with all his grand plans for world domination foiled—or aggravate him further. He was pretty sure Fenris couldn't hurt them here, wherever *here* was. So, yes, he wanted to aggravate him.

"The financial world? The *financial* world? There was no blood involved. Not a drop!"

"Well, some of the board meetings were brutal. If the members had had weapons, it would have been bloody." Declan obviously had no problem needling the huge wolf.

"Could have, would have... I don't give a raven's ass! You being mates I could have accepted, two uber alphas working together—not how it usually went, but doable. New times and all that. But you never killed *anybody!*" Fenris sounded shaken, the concept of refraining from killing others alien to his mindset of conquest and superiority.

"Well, how does the saying go? This is not a My Little Pony farm. We conquered a lot of companies and converted them into eco-friendly, ethical businesses, which help keep the planet you so desperately want to get under your rule inhabitable. If that's not good enough for you, get yourself some new uber alphas." Troy was getting aggressive. He wanted to go back to their mate, to love him properly now that the claiming was out of the way.

"I can't! That's the whole problem!" Fenris jumped in the air, his bulky head swinging from side to side in righteous outrage. "Do you think I would have put up with you if I had better options?"

"How charming," Declan muttered. Fenris kept raging.

"The rules say there can only be one uber alpha walking the Earth, two in your case, because the Norns have decided to make you *mates*. And I can't just kill you, because that has to happen through an adversary from this world. And by choosing Beaconville, it shall be damned for eons after Ragnarök has taken place because you made it impossible for me to convince anybody to go after you."

"Huh?" Declan looked at Troy.

"I guess he's referring to Mavis, Maribel, Jon, Amber and Emilia."

Fenris made a dirty sound. "Wolves have never formed allegiances with witches and vampires, not to mention the death messengers. *Nobody* wants to mess with any of them. And the demons…? Who mates with a demon? Ah, yes, I forgot, *you* do. Keeping me forever from putting the uber alpha on this planet I need to rule the world."

"Again, huh?" Declan was getting more confused by the second, as Troy could feel through their bond.

"I think it's because we're mated to Alerion now. Makes us close to immortal and damn near indestructible, which means no new uber alphas for Fenris." If there was a hint of glee in his voice, Troy was sure it was due to the strangeness of this place, warping sound as it pleased. Yes, that was it, definitely, because he wasn't gloating — no, no, not him. He was a mature adult, not some child, and… Who was he kidding? He was close to bursting from malicious pleasure at seeing the mighty, arrogant Fenris so dejected. Life could be so, so sweet. "Technically, we are now ruling an empire in addition to the financial world. As the mates of the King of all Demons, I'm sure we have some leadership responsibilities."

Fenris started twitching. It looked a lot like a child's wind-up toy gone crazy. "As mates! That's terrible! You should rule because you earned the right by wading through rivers of blood, not because you happen to sleep with the king!"

Troy had nothing to say to that. If there was a competition for the picture next to toxic masculinity in dictionaries, Fenris would be one of the top contenders — right up there with some of the nastier human rulers. "I think we're done here, Declan. There's nothing to be learned from *him*, and I want to close my arms around our mate."

"You took the words out of my mouth. How do we go back?"

Declan wasn't done speaking when the rocky landscape with Fenris started to fade. Apparently, whoever was in charge of sending the mates of demons to this non-world while their bodies changed had either realized there was nothing to be gained here or the process was finished. If he had to choose, Troy would take pain over talking to Fenris any day.

# Chapter Four

Alerion watched as his mates slowly regained consciousness. Their bodies were now marked in the demon tongue, making them look even more delectable in his eyes. Gingerly, he felt for the two bite marks on his neck. Despite the scales he hadn't tucked in again, his fingers brushed over the small ridges that had formed between the little holes his mates' teeth had made. He knew they were circled by gold, now forever part of the tattoos adorning his body.

Declan was the first to move, his lips in a grim line. He rolled his head on the cushion, baring his neck in the process. Alerion smiled. The mating bite Declan and Troy had given each other long before they met him was visible now, enhanced by the gold of their tattoos. Alerion briefly marveled at how he had managed to instinctively bite them on the other side of where they had marked each other. It might have been a miracle, magic or chance. He didn't care, just took it in stride because he now had mates. Two wonderful, beautiful, amazing mates, and he wouldn't feel alone ever again. Alerion was under no illusions that his job as king would become any easier just because he was now bound to the two werewolves, but it would make coming home all the sweeter. He was sure of it.

Troy opened his eyes, their amber color glowing for a moment, taking Alerion out of his pondering.

"Alerion?"

"I'm here, Troy. How are you feeling?"

"Like I've received a demon's poison — and I can't believe I'm saying this without any innuendo."

"You're innuendo personified, Troy." Declan's voice was gritty, and clearly interested, which in turn made Alerion's cock interested as well.

"Do I dare ask who you met in the world between?"

"You know where we went?" Declan looked surprised.

"I didn't go with you, if that's what you want to know. But I do know the mind of a demon mate goes to the world between to deal with the pain."

"Is that like another universe? Jon has told us a bit about them." Troy sat up, wriggling his butt over the expensive sheet to get closer to Alerion. It was an enticing sight.

"What?" Alerion had to admit he was a bit distracted.

"The world between. Is it like one of those universes Jon and Barion use as models for their computer game?" Troy was now snuggling up to him. Declan was coming up on his other side, his hands roaming freely over Alerion's chest, which did delicious things to the regions south of his navel.

"Computer game?"

Declan chuckled. "I think we have to stop touching our gorgeous mate if we want a coherent answer."

"Uhm, no. Hard pass. Answers are overrated, anyway. Let's get with the program." Troy lifted his leg to straddle Alerion, then grabbed Declan's hair to pull him in for a hot, messy three-way kiss. It was something they would have to practice, and Alerion was looking forward to it.

# Chapter Five

Troy woke because his wolf was telling him there was food—and intruders. *Intruders with food.* Which made them intruders who would live to see the end of the day instead of a decorative bloody smear on the walls of their mate's cabin-palace.

"Don't you think we're being pushy? They're newly mated after all." Troy recognized Jon's voice and groaned silently, knowing who else would be here. He only hoped they had kept it to family only and not brought the whole book club.

"No, it's not being pushy. It's surprising them with a tasty breakfast we labored hard to collect from all over the world in order to congratulate them on their mating." Barion, the asshole, sounding way too chipper for somebody who had celebrated his own mating only yesterday. Then again, maliciousness probably worked on him like caffeine.

"I still think we should just drop the food then leave them alone. It's the polite thing to do." Sammy, the best human in the world.

"No, *mo grah thu*, we need to check if our father is fine. Mating with two shifters is strenuous, and he's not as young as he used to be." Dre, being an absolute bastard, was obviously banking on them hearing him to rile them up. He was being successful, Troy realized when he felt his claws coming out. *Damn.*

"Oh, I hadn't thought about that. Do you think he needs medicine? Should we go back home and get some salve and…I don't know. What could help him if he's exhausted from, you know…sex?" *Sammy, still so innocent.* How could he not see what a deviant his mate was?

"I can assure you, Sammy, my dear boy, I don't need any medicine. But my brat of a son needs a good spanking. Old? I'll give you old!" Alerion sounded more amused than annoyed and winked at Troy when he turned to look at Alerion, who was perched on his elbows between Troy and Declan, who was slowly getting up as well.

"What's going on?" Troy found it fascinating how Declan could be so relaxed with intruders in their home. Well, familiar intruders who both their wolves had accepted as pack the moment they'd met them, but still creatures not supposed to be here on their first morning as a mated throuple.

"My sons and sons-in-law are here, presumably to bring us breakfast." Alerion leaned down to Declan to give him a kiss on the mouth that turned dirty fast. Troy hadn't known he was whining until Alerion broke the kiss with Declan to give him the same attention.

"I think they're kissing. Isn't that sweet?" Sammy said again, who still hadn't gotten used to his enhanced hearing or any of the other perks being the mate of a demon brought.

"They're newly mated. Of course they're kissing. Be grateful it's just that." Barion snorted with suppressed laughter. Troy wasn't sure, but he thought he heard an elbow connecting with a hard stomach, followed by an *umph*.

"Be nice, Barion. We're here to congratulate them, not aggravate the hell out of them." Ah, Jon was the nicest zombie Troy had ever met. "You can do that starting next week when their honeymoon is over." He was also turning into quite the little bitch now that he was mated.

"Why don't you set the table while my mates and I make ourselves presentable?" Alerion again, amusement dancing in his eyes. Troy knew he could get lost in those deep green eyes if they had the time, but breakfast was waiting, and Declan was already leaving the bed.

After they were presentable — which took them long enough to trigger another round of good-natured ribbing spoken too loudly to not be meant to be overheard — they joined the terrible four in the open kitchen where they had set a roughly hewn wooden table. The unknown interior designer had probably gone for 'lumberjack chic', not taking into account that even a roughhewn table could look like it cost a few thousand dollars in the right surroundings — or perhaps it had been on purpose. Troy knew shit about interior design.

The table was covered with all kinds of delicious food from all over the world. There were French crepes and croissants, fresh strawberries from wherever in the world they were ripe at the moment, fresh rolls from Germany, if Troy wasn't mistaken — he had by now participated in enough breakfasts with Sammy and Dre to know what to expect—two jars of strawberry marmalade from Mavis and Maribel, always a treat, as well as an entire plate of their chocolate chip cookies. There was also yogurt, different cheeses and an interesting-smelling sausage, two huge mugs with coffee just the way he and Declan loved it—no doubt made by Sammy personally, the only person who ever got it right—as well as a third mug with hot chocolate spiced with chili, which was apparently for Alerion.

They all sat down, and for a few glorious moments absolute silence reigned while everybody loaded their plates.

"I would ask how the claiming went, but as we all can see the mating bites and the tattoos, I guess that's redundant." Dre looked at their naked torsos.

Troy shrugged. From the corner of his eye, he saw Declan winking while Alerion, who was seated between them, something their wolves had been adamant about, looked so happy it made Troy's heart beat faster.

Alerion had explained that when a demon was newly mated, their mate presented themselves naked so all the other demons could see the tattoos. Naked had, of course, been out of the question. Nobody got to see the goods but them, but neither Troy nor Declan were shy about their bodies, and their wolves were more than happy to show off their mating scars and the tattoos. And because Alerion truly was the best mate ever, he too had kept his shirt off, though Troy wasn't entirely sure it was to show solidarity. He had a suspicion that their mate didn't want them to have the advantage when it came to getting naked again. That was absolutely fine by Troy, because Alerion was a feast for the eyes, not to mention he could totally get behind this kind of reasoning.

"It went well." Alerion winked before he sipped some of his hot chocolate with a soft groan. "I have to say, Sammy, this new recipe is even better than the one before."

Sammy blushed at the compliment. "I found this old Aztec recipe for hot chocolate online. Dre helped me locate the right cocoa beans, and from there it was a bit of trial and error. If Barion hadn't helped, I probably wouldn't have managed to get it right."

"Barion helped you to make cocoa? That sounds... wrong." Declan shoved a strawberry into his mouth and Troy had to suppress the urge to kiss him just to taste the sweet berry juice mixed with his mate's own flavor.

"Hey, I can be very helpful!" Barion threw the stone of an apricot at Declan, who expertly ducked out of the way.

"Yes, Barion was the best! He..." Sammy stopped abruptly, slapping his hand over his mouth to keep himself from speaking while going as red as a tomato. They were the typical signs of him skirting the very edge of blurting out something he shouldn't. Sensing blood, Troy dug deeper.

"Barion did what, Sammy?"

Sammy's eyes widened in panic, and he looked first at Dre, then Barion for help. It was highly suspicious, which had Troy's wolf taking notice. The little human was hiding something...a secret. Getting secrets out of Sammy was fun, because he always got adorably flustered when he let them slip—and he was already close. Troy could practically smell it, as could Declan, obviously, who joined Troy in the verbal hunt.

"Yes, Sammy, what did Barion do?"

Sammy made a squeaking sound and started sliding down his chair and under the table. Before he reached the edge of it with his head, Alerion stopped him.

"Troy, Declan, don't tease my poor son-in-law. He's defenseless, as you well know." His chastising tone would have probably been more intimidating if it hadn't been laced with pure lust. All of a sudden, Alerion was radiating Daddy-vibes, and Troy was this close to calling him 'Sir'.

"Sammy, dear, you did nothing wrong. On the contrary, you caught yourself before anything bad could happen, and I'm so proud of you," Alerion said.

Under the praise, a smile blossomed on Sammy's lips while Dre helped him back into an upright position.

"Now, Declan and Troy are part of the family. Barion, if you choose to share your secret, now would be a good time before my two mates explode from curiosity. If you don't wish them to know, that's fine as well. The subject will be dropped." Hearing his mate talk with so much authority had Troy's wolf panting. His tail was wagging like crazy, and he was urging Troy to roll onto his back so their mate could assert his dominance properly, in a definitely sexual way. Judging from what he got from Declan, he was very much on board with this scenario.

"Teasing them sounds like fun." Barion grinned. It reminded Troy of the current topic, which had him torn. Thinking sexy thoughts about his mate or finding out about a secret? *Decisions, decisions.*

"Barion!" Declan whined. He had come to a conclusion much faster than Troy, it seemed.

Alerion looked darkly at his youngest son, who threw his hands in the air, his claws out for emphasis.

"Fine. Okay, this is a secret, obviously, but I'm telling you because I know you're going to pester Sammy until he cracks, and that's just not fair."

"We wouldn't!" Troy and Declan spoke in unison, knowing full well they wouldn't have been able to withstand temptation, especially if it potentially meant a punishment from Alerion. Troy's wolf started panting again.

"You can't tell anybody else." Barion sounded so serious that Troy and Declan responded in kind. There was a time for making fun and teasing, and there was a time for being all grown up and responsible, which was now.

"We won't." Again, they spoke in unison. Troy felt Alerion's hand on his nape, which sent a shudder of happy anticipation through his body. A secret *and* sex with their mate. The day couldn't get any better.

"Fine." Barion paused for dramatic effect. "Now, as you know, demons are a great species, far superior to all others and full of wondrous surprises."

"Full of shit is more like it." That was Jon, who got a smacking kiss for his comment.

"You love me for it, and you know it."

"If your great secret is your tendency to brag without being able to back it up, then we already know." Declan took the words right out of Troy's mouth.

Barion shot both of them an angry glare. "I'm doing a great reveal here, so shut up, assholes."

"Language, son." Alerion admonished.

"I hate to tell you this, babe, but your skills for great reveals leave room for improvement." Jon kissed

Barion's cheek to take the sting out of his words. It seemed to work, because the frown that had been forming between Barion's brows vanished almost instantly.

Sammy sighed. "I'm so sorry. I should have never brought this up."

"Oh, no, *mo grah thu*. This is sooo much fun," Dre said.

"Okay, so back to the great reveal." Barion's voice was almost a monotone now. "Every demon has a secret special talent. Mine is I can show every moment in the past with complete accuracy, exactly how it happened. Also, I can bend time for about five minutes."

Troy stared at Barion. "You can show the past? And you're not working as a homicide detective or PI or something similarly cool?"

"Wow, Troy is right. I've never thought about that!" Sammy clapped his hands. "We have to go to London and find out who Jack the Ripper was!"

"No, first we go to Dallas, Texas, and see who killed Kennedy!" Declan was fired up. Troy could feel it through their bond.

"Slow down, *mo grah thu*. Remember what we talked about concerning Barion's talent?" Dre was holding Sammy's hands to prevent him from whisking his plate to the ground. It took a moment, then Sammy deflated, and it was like seeing a puppy being kicked.

"I'm sorry, Barion. I'm respecting your boundaries and wondering who it was is way more fun than knowing." He looked at Dre for approval, and his mate gave him a soft kiss.

"Excellent, my love. I promise we can go to the library later today to look for all the old documents regarding the case." Troy had to give it to Dre. The man knew how to make his mate happy. Sammy was peppering him with kisses.

Troy returned his attention to Barion. "This means you showed Sammy how the Aztecs made chocolate so he could copy the recipe for Alerion."

Barion nodded. "We spent hours in that temple in the Andes, until he was sure he had all the details."

"You're a great brother-in-law," Jon praised his mate.

"I know... That's just me." Barion looked smug.

Troy could feel the gears in his head turning. He turned to Alerion. "Do you have a secret talent as well?"

Alerion winked. "I do."

"But they don't know?" Troy gestured with his thumb at Dre, Sammy, Jon and Barion.

"They don't, but perhaps it's time to tell them. Do you want to know?" The question was for everybody in the room, and this time Sammy's cutlery clattered to the floor.

Alerion smiled indulgently at his son-in-law before he took both Troy's and Declan's hands. "My special talent is that I know every dance in existence."

Troy felt his mouth forming an O. He had definitely expected something else. "Every dance in existence?"

"Yes." Alerion sounded so proud.

"Like every dance on Earth? That has ever been danced?" Sammy was leaning half over the table, his red T-Shirt with the rainbow cupcakes dipping into the bowl of yogurt.

"Every dance on Earth that has ever been danced."

"That's... Wow!" Sammy got back up with the help of Dre, yogurt dripping from his shirt, adding an interesting white splash to the explosion of color already going on there.

"Troy and I love to dance." Declan's eyes were bright with happiness.

Troy could already see the three of them swaying to a romantic song or going crazy doing a samba.

"That's an interesting talent, Dad." Barion cocked his head. "And has about the same usefulness as mine."

"Don't say that. Both your talents are great! You can literally relive history, and Alerion can teach us the dances throughout the ages. I'm so excited. We have to start some kind of history night, like the book club. We could agree on a certain area or era or point in time and go there and see what it was like, and the crowning glory is we get to dance in the end." Sammy's cheeks had gone all red while he was hopping on his seat, no doubt already planning their first history night.

Troy shuddered. He was all for keeping the past where it belonged — behind them — though he assumed that was mainly because his and Declan's past wasn't much to write home about, at least before they had decided to move to Beaconville. He could see a certain appeal when viewed through Sammy's lens of absolute excitement about learning for learning's sake, but not enough to develop a real interest.

"A history night sounds interesting, Sammy." The indulgent smile Alerion seemed to have reserved for Sammy was back. "Though I'm afraid more than once a month won't be possible for me. My demons are quite adventurous at the moment, and I do have two mates now." The smile turned hungry, reminding Troy they hadn't had sex in at least six hours.

"May I ask what your talent is, Dre?" Declan leaned forward a bit. Trust his inquisitive mate to not forget the third demon in their midst. And as much as Troy wanted to get rid of their unannounced guests to return to bed, he was curious as well.

"Can you smell colors? Or go into the future?" Troy tossed these things out randomly, just to tease Dre a bit. The huge demon made a face.

"That would be nice. I'm afraid my talent isn't as cool as Dad's and Barion's."

"Don't say that, my beloved. I love your talent." Sammy had put a hand on Dre's forearm, rubbing gentle circles with this thumb while looking at Dre with absolute love in his eyes. It was sickeningly sweet and made Troy's wolf resolve to kill anybody who dared to make Sammy sad. He could feel the same notion from Declan, and they shared a look. This was new. Their wolves had always been protective of Sammy, always willing to spill blood on his behalf, but never before had the feeling been so intense. Perhaps it was because Alerion obviously loved Sammy as well. If he were hurt, their mate would be hurt. The wolves couldn't let that happen.

"Come on, Dre. Don't leave us hanging." Declan clapped his hands once.

Dre sighed. "Fine, my talent is chaos."

Silence.

"Huh?" Declan stared at Dre.

"I have no active control over it, obviously, since it's, you know, chaos, but it yields to me, you could say."

"Which means?" Troy looked expectantly at Dre. He still didn't understand.

"Well, I either cause chaos or make it cease, depending on the circumstances and my intent."

"That's what Grann meant when she said you make everything blurry!" Jon snapped his fingers. "It really worried her, you know, that she couldn't see when you're near. Something about you distorting some lines?"

Jon was a computer genius, no doubt, but when it came to magic, he had the attention span of a toddler on a sugar high. Then again, if Grann was the Witch Queen of New Orleans and also a blessed child of Papa Legba, worrying about magical details was probably low on the list. If Grann couldn't deal with it, Jon surely wouldn't be able to.

"Uh, yes. Chaos tends to fuck with possibilities. There's even a mathematical side to it. Quirion explained it to me once...in detail." Dre shuddered.

Until the day before, Troy had never met Dre's and Barion's older brother, and to say the demon was intense was putting it mildly. Where Sammy's love for history and learning was endearing, Quirion seemed to take it as serious as a heart attack. He also gave the impression that he was willing to take heads if the sciences weren't treated with respect.

"I really don't know which of your talents is the best." Declan winked. "Though I tend toward Alerion's. Knowing all dances? That's just great."

"You're heavily biased. I think Barion's talent is the best." Jon took the last strawberry from the plate. Barion gave him a kiss on the top of his head.

"No, Dre's is the absolute best," Sammy said with conviction. "Though the other two are close seconds."

"No favorites there?" Barion gave Sammy the puppy-dog eyes.

"No. I'd never be able to choose. I love you both too much."

And there it was. Among all the banter and ribbing, Sammy would say something totally earnest and absolutely sweet, making the recipients all teary. He could see Alerion sniffling next to him.

"As we love you." Alerion reached over the table to pat Sammy's hand.

"Before things get too emotional, what about you two?" Dre was rubbing Sammy's back, blinking fast, no doubt to hide the suspicious sheen in his eyes.

"What about us two?" Troy feigned innocence. They had kept their uber alpha identity under tight wraps. He hadn't been surprised that Mavis and Maribel had known, few things managed to evade the two witches, but the rest of their friends had been clueless. Maybe Emilia had had some suspicions, though never anything substantial. They had made sure of it. Troy glanced at Declan, who nodded. They were mated now, which made the men sitting at the table with them not only pack but also immediate family. They deserved to know, especially since the council would surely start stirring shit up. It was just something Troy knew in his bones. Under no circumstances would they pass up a chance at extorting them one way or another. It was how they worked.

"Well, as you already heard yesterday, Declan and I? We're uber alphas."

"You make it sound like that's a bad thing." Jon's brows were furrowed.

"Well, considering we were born to fight against each other to the death, it kind of is." Troy smiled weakly when he felt Alerion's hand on his nape. A quick glance confirmed he was doing the same with Declan. Having mates was simply the best.

"To the death?" Sammy's eyes were big as saucers. "That's just mean!"

Leave it to Sammy to put things in simple yet accurate words.

"Yes, it was pretty mean. Fenris, the god of werewolves, isn't known for being nice." Troy lifted a hand to keep Sammy from saying something again. If he did, Troy wasn't sure he wouldn't do something stupid, like start crying or wrap the adorable human in a hug to absorb all his sweetness. "So, Fenris is an asshole, and he has this delusion that a werewolf should rule the world. It didn't work out for long with Alexander the Great, and I think we can all agree Napoleon wasn't a success story, either. Anyway, there are always two uber alphas born so they can fight to the death when they come of age. Fenris has this weird notion that just because you are born a certain way, you shouldn't get everything handed on a silver platter. You have to wade through blood to prove your worth."

"Sounds utterly charming." Dre's lips formed a grim line.

"Oh, it is. As you can imagine, our first eighteen years on this earth weren't exactly fun." Troy glanced at Declan, who nodded gravely. "We both knew what was waiting for us, but even when we were young, we had this gut feeling, I guess you can call it, that things wouldn't go the way everybody was expecting. We both fought to get the best education possible, arguing that if we should rule the world, we needed to understand how it worked first."

"We both went into finance and law." Declan took over. "Being an uber alpha comes with a lot of perks. We're not only stronger than all other werewolves — faster, too — but we're also pretty smart. I don't think this is something Fenris has done on purpose. To him, brute strength is more than enough, but I guess it comes with the territory. Anyway, we were prodigies, had our degrees by seventeen and had both already started our own businesses."

"Even though you knew you'd be fighting to the death at eighteen? You're both so brave!" Sammy had a death grip on Dre's hand, who was leaning close to his mate to soothe him.

Troy cleared his throat. "We both were optimistic. We didn't really have a contingency plan, because as uber alphas, we weren't able to hide, so running was out of the question and as much as we tried, we weren't able to find the other. The council made sure of that."

"The Shifter Council?" Barion frowned. "Last time I had contact with them, they were a bunch of boring old farts so stuck up on their own importance they wouldn't have been able to know a decision for the good of shifters if it spit them in the eye."

"A very colorful, very correct summary of the council." Declan grinned. "I don't know when your encounter with them took place, but nothing has changed. Well, perhaps they have become even worse. Anyway, on the night before the duel, which neither of us had any inclination to fight, we were both visited by Fenris, who made this tedious speech about superiority and werewolf strength and ruling the world by bathing it in blood and blah, blah, blah. We later compared notes, and he had the exact same speech for both of us. To him, we're just tools." Declan's eyes sparkled. "Broken tools."

"Yeah." Troy showed all his teeth. "We met in the ring, and instead of witnessing one of us tearing the other to shreds, we took one whiff and knew we were mates. The council was very unhappy, and Fenris told us last night while Alerion's poison changed our bodies, that the Norns had cheated him. We think it's rather funny. The council kept hounding us, declaring we had to take over the world together. We finally managed to get them off our hides by threatening to kill them all and by moving to Beaconville. They've left us mostly alone, just a call now and then, whining about how we're not fulfilling our destiny and similar nonsense."

"They're not leaving you alone now?" Alerion was too perceptive for his own good.

"At the moment, things are still quiet. But they will find out about our mating—much later, if we have anything to say about it—and once they do, they won't be able to withstand temptation. We can't say what they're going to do or how they're going to react to us having another alpha mate instead of a docile omega who can become our breeding machine." Troy shrugged. "There's not much they can do except annoy us. We're too strong, you're the freaking demon king and we're based in Beaconville. I don't see any major problems." Troy was sure the council would come up with something, but that was hopefully way in the future. Right at the moment, they had a mating to celebrate.

"You don't think they'll come to Beaconville to threaten Sammy?" Jon looked worried.

Even though Sammy was now a demon's mate and therefore pretty much indestructible, he was still the weak link, simply because he always saw the good in people. He wouldn't think twice about talking to somebody from the council or even inviting them to his home. It was his greatest asset, as well as his weakness, his willingness to give people chances—even the ones who could turn him into a toad, like Mavis and Maribel, rip him to pieces, like Troy, Declan, Amelia, Amber and Jon could or had attempted to sacrifice him to a demon, like Milo had. Hell, he hadn't even shied away from letting Dre into his life, a demon! Sammy's naivety was the reason they had this wonderful, if unusual, family. If anything happened to him, he would also be the reason for utter destruction.

"They won't. No paranormal with harmful intent ever comes to Beaconville, if you haven't noticed yet. No paranormal comes to Beaconville, period. I'm not saying they won't try anything, but they will be very careful. Us being uber alphas means all shifters have to do our bidding. They can't refuse an order from us. If needs be, we'll say nobody can touch Sammy or anybody else in our family."

"A wonderful idea, Troy." Alerion nodded in his direction. "Now let's not be pessimistic. We know there is the potential of a threat, but before it becomes reality, they have to realize we're mated. How long did you say haven't you heard from them?"

Troy looked at Declan, who shrugged. "I think it's been almost five years now. Before that, they didn't contact us for two years, probably because they thought the silent treatment would break us. Hah!"

"No immediate danger then. Let's hope they keep their radio silence. Now, Dre, Barion, Sammy, Jon, as much as I love you and as wonderful as this breakfast has been, I really need to be alone with my mates. We have things to discuss." Alerion managed to look perfectly serious while saying this.

Dre snickered. "No worries, Dad. We were freshly mated, too. Go back and break the bed. We'll see you in Beaconville?"

"Yes. Expect us tomorrow…in the evening." Alerion put a hand of each of his mates' thighs. "I'm afraid I can't be unavailable for much longer."

"Don't worry, Dad. We can keep an eye on things." Barion got up, dragging Jon with him. "Take the next four days off. We'll holler if there's a problem."

Troy felt Alerion's grip on his thigh tightening. "You're the best sons ever. Thank you."

"Yeah, thank you." Troy was already panting from the flood of pheromones in the air.

"Why is it smelling so sweet all of a sudden?" Sammy sniffed around.

"No particular reason, *mo grah thu*. Let's go." Dre nodded at them, grabbed Sammy, sliced space and time and off they went. Barion and Jon followed with a wave, and they were alone again.

Alerion got up. He had started shifting into his demon form, the black scales rippling over his torso. "Race you to the bedroom." And off he went.

Troy and Declan looked at each other, growled and sprinted after their mate.

They had four hopefully uninterrupted days.

They would make the most of it.

# Chapter Six

"Do we really have to go work?" Declan was whining like a little pup, and he knew it. Troy shot him a scathing look.

"I'm no more inclined to dive back into the world of finance than you are, but our mate is already off doing *his* job, which leaves no reason for us not to do *ours*."

They both growled lowly when they remembered Alerion's hasty departure from the apartment. It was their first morning back after four blissfully sexy days at the cabin-palace. At times, Declan had wished time would stop and they could stay there forever. Unfortunately, reality was a mean little bitch who came knocking at their door without the least bit of mercy.

Alerion was now dealing with another 'demons-just-wanna-have-fun' emergency. This time in Budapest, which meant their mate was thousands of miles away from them. If he hadn't been such a powerful being, their wolves would have had a lot more to say about it. Declan knew the wolves could be as old-fashioned as mummies from the desert, which didn't change the fact that mates had to be protected at all times—just in case being an eight-foot demon with lethal claws and fangs longer than Declan's forearm, backed up by scales only demon claws could rip through after several tries wasn't enough to keep said mate safe. Wolves weren't known for their logic, either. Logic was for weaklings who couldn't rip annoying people in half without even breaking a sweat.

Speaking of which, they had yet to see their mate's full demon form. So far, the eight feet were what Declan had deduced from seeing Dre and Barion, who were both well over seven feet. As their father, Alerion surely would be taller, wouldn't he? His wolf started wagging his tail just imagining running with such a supreme predator, not to mention mate with him.

"Uh, Declan, I'm pretty sure I know what you're thinking at the moment, your pheromones are clogging up my nose, and I'm not saying I can't get behind your train of thought, but I'm also not going to the board meeting with a hard-on big enough to rip my zipper."

Declan left the dream world where he and his mates were having naked fun to stare at Troy. His wolf mate was indeed showing an impressive erection, rivalling his own. He sighed.

"Cold shower? Because I think taking care of it won't help."

Troy was already turning on his heels, heading for the bathroom and showing off his tight-as-sin ass, which looked so delicious when Alerion's cock was balls-deep in it.

*Down, boy. We have work to do. Fun comes after.*

His wolf growled, not happy with Declan's reasoning. Too bad they couldn't abandon their businesses forever. He was reaching for the zipper of his own slacks when Troy's phone started ringing with Cannibal Corpse's *Decency Defied*, the ringtone they had assigned for the council. As Troy had explained during their celebratory breakfast with the terrible four, the old farts hadn't bothered them in over five years, after Troy and Declan had made it very clear they wouldn't hesitate to shred every last member of the council into tiny little pieces if they weren't left alone.

It had, of course, been a bluff. Despite being perfectly able to cause such a bloodbath, Troy and Declan would never *ever* contemplate getting that much blood on their expensive suits. And neither of them wanted to pluck bits of fur from between their teeth for weeks. No, the shredding would have taken place on another level, where Declan and Troy would have ruined the council financially.

Knowing that bunch of whackos would always be a threat, they had started early to buy into the companies the individual members owned or had a part in — always in disguise as not to draw attention to their very evil Plan B. By now, they — and Emilia, the vampire had been a great help in getting the deciding percent for more than one company — were able to pull the financial rug from under the council members' feet within days. Most of them would be completely ruined immediately, and having this advantage was what mollified their wolves more than keeping their teeth fur-free. In the end, it was a question of perception, as always.

Troy had fished out his cell and eyed it with clear dismay. Their options were twofold. They could choose to ignore the call, knowing full well the council would keep calling until they spoke to them, or they could get the unpleasantness behind them. The good news was a cold shower was no longer needed, because there was no greater erection killer in the world than the mere prospect of talking to the council. A hot shower might be in order after the discussion to get rid of the slimy feeling all over their skin, though.

Declan steeled himself and nodded at Troy, who rolled his eyes, bared his teeth at the cell which hadn't stopped blasting the violent notes out, and hit the green icon.

"Finally... What took you so long?" The voice of Elder Simarl quaked through the speaker like a frog on the verge of choking.

"Good day to you, too, Elder Simarl. It's always a pleasure to talk to you." Troy's voice was as dry as the Sahara Desert. His lips twitched in the secure knowledge that any and all sarcasm was completely lost on the pompous elder.

"What pleasure? Talking to you gives me hives." The elder was also rude as fuck, because apparently once you reached a certain age, saying whatever was on your mind became mandatory—which was charming when Mavis and Maribel did it, because they were classy as fuck, and terrible when the elder did it, because next to him even a pigsty would have looked like an evening at the Met.

"Anyway, I'm calling to congratulate you on finding your mate. We will hold a ceremony at the end of this week to celebrate your mate and to introduce her to the council as the future bearer of your offspring."

Declan and Troy shared a look. "First of all, how do you know we've found our third? It's only been five days, and we'd know if we'd told you. You're so far down our list of people to inform, however, that we probably would have never gotten around to making that call." Troy huffed.

Declan gave him the thumbs up. Getting in as many jabs as possible while talking to the council was a game they had invented shortly after their mating.

The elder *tsk*ed. "You're the uber alphas. Every werewolf in existence knew it the moment you bit your mate. Haven't you learned anything?"

"Must have slipped our minds." Troy shuddered. "Just to be clear, you only felt it when we bit our mate?"

"Of course. Nobody wants to be present when two males get physical. Though I think it's better now that you have a female. I hope she's a decent omega from a good line?"

Elder Simarl was also a raging homophobe, on top of being an annoying, arrogant rude fuck. The man was just a pile of pleasantness.

*Do we tell him?* Declan formed with his lips. The mean glint in his mate's eyes was answer enough. With a deceptively smooth tone, Troy started.

"I can assure you, Elder Simarl, *he* is not only of a good line, but a royal one."

"Royalty? I'm glad you got at least that right, though I can't imagine where you'd find somebody. Did you say *he*?" The elder's voice had reached an unpleasant pitch at the end of the sentence. Declan gave Troy a thumbs up. This was shaping up to be fun.

"Yes. What did you think? We're very much gay, Elder. Giving us a female mate would have been futile, don't you agree?"

For a few precious moments, there was only sputtering at the other end of the line, igniting the hope the elder would simply pass out from indignation. They had no such luck, though. Simarl cleared his throat, the rustling of clothes being adjusted could be heard, then the Elder's voice was back, as jarring as always.

"I should have expected this. You said he's from a royal line? Care to give me more details so we don't make any mistakes during the ceremony?"

Declan's jaw hurt he was smiling so broadly. This was going to be soooo much fun. Troy winked.

"Of course, Elder. His name and title are Alerion, King of All Demons. As for this ceremony, I'm pretty sure we won't be able to make it. Seeing as our mate is a king, he has a lot of responsibility, as you probably can imagine. Also, we're not overly keen on spending precious time with you lot. I'd suggest you schedule this ceremony for the eve of never, at 'just-forget-about-it o'clock."

This time they didn't hear any sputtering nor rustling. The line had just gone deadly silent. Troy's finger was already hovering over the red icon to end the call, when the elder started shrieking. "You mated with the demon king? How will there be offspring to rule, when you're mated to another alpha male? *Three* alphas? That shouldn't be possible! How can you do that to your own people? Your pack? What about your responsibilities?"

"Uh, we don't have a pack, remember? We left this whole circus behind when you decided to send us into a fight against each other. We're very happy with our mate, thank you very much, because our perception of being an alpha clearly is very different from yours. We never intended to sire offspring, mainly because we don't want any poor pups to be poisoned with your outdated ideas about pretty much everything. You have congratulated us, which wasn't necessary, now please leave us alone."

Troy hit the red icon before the elder could launch into another rant about alphas and duty and whatever nonsense he thought Declan and Troy should conform to.

"Wow, he took that worse than I thought." Troy was already laughing.

"Not bad enough. I had hoped the mention of Alerion would shut him up completely. You know, a kind of 'swallow his tongue' scenario."

"Hope springs eternal. Do you think we got rid of them for good this time?"

Declan shook his head. "You know how they are. They're going to brood a bit until they find a way to spin this to their liking. If I were a betting man, I'd say they next demand we use the demon army at our mate's beck and call to conquer the world."

Troy's eyes lit up in interest. They weren't betting men. Oh no, they were betting wolves — strictly between them, the currency being blow jobs. "I say they try to get their hands on the money, claiming some shit like the mate of the uber alphas has to hand over his assets to the council for safekeeping."

Sadly, this idea wasn't as outlandish as it might have sounded to a sane person's ears. The council had left sanity so far behind that it wasn't even a distant speck on the horizon anymore.

Declan grabbed Troy's hand. "Usual odds?"

Troy hesitated. "We have a mate now. Should we involve him? In the bet, I mean, not the madness that is the council. He's got enough on his platter with his demons."

"Let's ask him to be the referee. And if the council comes up with something totally different, he gets the blow jobs."

"Deal." They sealed it with a deep kiss before they decided to take that shower to get rid of the dirty feeling talking to the council always brought on.

Once they were on the way to their car to get to the board meeting, Troy started tapping the side of his thigh. "What do we get Alerion as a mating gift?"

"Oh." Declan had been so busy basking in the happy glow of sex with both his mates, he'd totally forgotten about the mating gift. It was a tradition among werewolves to present a mate with something of value that also had a deeper meaning for the people involved. The problem here was, with Alerion being the King of all Demons, he probably had everything he wanted — certainly all the valuables money could buy.

"It'll have to be something really special." Declan looked around in the alley where they had parked their car. The great thing about Beaconville was that it was small enough for everybody to know that their car was off-limits, even though the custom-made BMW was pure temptation for a thief.

"What do we know about Alerion?" Troy got the keys out of his pocket.

Declan thought hard. "He's great in bed. The sex is beyond hot. He looks like a god. His tongue is pure bliss, his dick to die for." That was about as far as their exploration of their mate had gone. New mates tended to have tunnel vision for a while. Troy chuckled.

"Perhaps a little something for his dick then? Jewelry?"

"I'm not sure he can have jewelry. I mean, we can't because of the shift. I can't imagine it's different for him."

"True. But imagine... No, no reason to get worked up." Troy shook his head vehemently.

"What else...?"

The soft rustling behind them made them both perk their ears. It was followed by a moment's silence, as if whoever was creeping up on them was trying to make sure they hadn't been spotted. Well, tough luck. To get the drop on two werewolves, even when they were distracted, was almost impossible.

Declan's muscles tensed, ready to pounce.

The shriek, followed by a hiss, made him jump over a foot in the air. Troy wasn't faring any better. He just covered his fright up better by landing smoothly on the Beemer's hood. Another shriek rent the air and was cut off abruptly enough for their inner predators to know what had happened. There was more rustling behind the trash bins at the end of the alley, then a deep, unholy yowl of triumph resounded.

A huge red tom marched from behind the dumpsters, carrying a rat in his muzzle, a big rat—so big, in fact, that Declan wondered if he had missed the reactor accident that had led to its growth. The tom eyed them with the arrogance of a predator who knew he was the most badass around. Usually animals were intimidated by them, sensing their wolves and keeping their distance. This tom, though, didn't change direction. It sauntered right up to them, the rat dangling around its front like a puppet on a string. Declan and Troy exchanged a look. No words were needed. The perfect gift. They had found it.

"We don't have time now. Let's get this board meeting over with, then we can go looking for him."

The tom, who looked a lot like Greebo from Terry Pratchett's *Discworld* with his missing ear and the countless scars, paraded past the BMW before he left the alley with a mocking twitch of his long tail, which was missing patches of fur.

"You think we'll find him again?"

Troy rolled his eyes.

Yes, it was a stupid question. That tom was clearly at home here. He wouldn't leave his territory, not as long as there was such big prey running around. He was the perfect present for Alerion, something unique their mate wouldn't be getting for himself or from just anybody, and he wouldn't be going anywhere anytime soon. Satisfied with their plans for the day, Declan followed Troy into the car to make a few board members tremble.

# Chapter Seven

"That was fun." Troy killed the Beemer's engine, cracking his knuckles. Making self-entitled board members who spent more time at the golf course than at work tremble in their seats was a great way to spend a day. His wolf was still a bit miffed that they hadn't chased Rubio Alvarez Montgomery III through the city until he perished from exhaustion. As tempting as the idea had been while listening to the man droning on and on about how important it was to raise the board members' wages while cutting those of the workers, it would have been bad style. Plus, the arrogant twit didn't deserve being the one who outed the paranormal world to humans. Putting him in his place — far away from the board — would be fun of a different kind as soon as they talked to their lawyer. All those pesky rules were tiresome, but Troy could appreciate the idea behind them — keeping people safe. Anyway, they had bigger fish — or cats — to fry. Alerion hadn't said when he would be back home, and in an ideal world, Troy and Declan would be able to present their mate with the tom as his mating gift.

On their way back to Beaconville, they had stopped at a pet shop and bought everything from cat food to a litter box that could only have been posher if it had running water, as well as a collar sparkling with rhinestones. As soon as the tom got used to wearing it, they would of course order one with real diamonds. Only the best for the mating gift.

Now all they had to do was find the tom, catch him and get him back to their apartment. As uber alphas, that shouldn't be a problem at all.

Troy looked at Declan, who was already partly shifted, another perk of being an uber. Normal werewolves couldn't do that. Declan's wolf nose twitched, which looked funny in his still almost-human face. Troy was so used to seeing his mate and himself in various states of part-shift that the image of a badly done flesh puzzle didn't faze him in the least, though he could understand how humans might find it scary. He let his nose shift as well, following Declan's example and taking in the scents in the alley. They had both gotten a whiff of the tom in the morning, which made following his scent easy. Out of the alley, around the apartment, into another, even narrower alley. It was fascinating how Beaconville had all these broad, friendly streets and such a maze of small, dingy, dark pathways permeating the town like the mycelium of a super-creepy mushroom.

Declan lifted his head, scenting the air, before he bent down, taking in the scents closer to the ground. The dead rat had left a path of slowly setting decay, and parts of it had to still be somewhere close, because the aroma was strong. A low rustling had both of them freezing. Their prey was near. Declan slowly swiveled his head in the direction the rustling had come from. Two large dumpsters painted in vomit green shielded the tom from them. Troy felt his wolf coming to the surface. It understood hunting. It understood getting a mating gift. It was completely on board.

"Shh!" Declan looked at him with narrowed eyes.

It took Troy a moment to realize he was snarling lowly. Clamping a hand over his mouth, he shut up. "Sorry!"

Declan shrugged. Movement behind the dumpster had them on high alert again. The tom came sauntering from behind it, staring at them with its gorgeous green eyes. Troy felt his wolf getting ready to pounce. As if he had read Troy's mind, the tom hissed, arching his back and fluffing out his tail. Troy had to admit it was an impressive display.

Unfortunately, his wolf saw it as an invitation to have a friendly challenge. The hair at his nape grew, forming a blade along his spine, pushing his thousand-dollar shirt out in an uncomfortable fashion. One look at Declan and he knew his mate wasn't doing any better. The tom fluffed his fur a little more, causing their wolves to do the same, which in turn made both of them wriggle, because the friction between cloth and fur itched like crazy. This seemed to amuse the tom— Troy would swear on everything that was holy that the damn cat was doing it on purpose—who started spitting while swiping the air with his front claws. Before Troy could intervene or even process what was happening, his and Declan's wolves were pushing through, showing their fangs and claws while growling menacingly.

The tom was duly impressed.

He sat down and started licking his ass.

The wolves both whined. They felt something was very wrong and couldn't understand why the little red ball of fur — for werewolves, anything smaller than a cow was little — didn't run. After the posturing came the chase. Everybody knew that. Why did the tom not follow the proper protocol?

He was now licking his front paw, not even looking at them anymore.

Troy looked at Declan, who seemed to be as lost as he was.

"Perhapsch we schould...." Declan shook his head, made his fangs retreat and started again. "Perhaps we should try to pet him?"

He made the three steps that separated them from the street cat, crouched down and extended his hand.

"Ouch!"

Declan jumped back so quickly that he landed on his ass, cradling his hand to his chest. The coppery scent of blood filled the air. The tom had stopped licking his paws. He was now looking nonchalantly at the claws that had drawn Declan's blood.

Troy was torn between wanting to eviscerate the arrogant feline for hurting his mate and laughing his ass off because said mate was still whining about the scratches that had to have healed by now.

A throat was cleared behind them.

Troy smiled broadly and turned to Alerion, who was standing at the entrance to the alley in all his dark glory, his wonderful scent overlaying the stink of the dumpsters.

"What are you two up to?"

Declan jumped to his feet, holding out his injured hand to the demon. As Troy had predicted, the scratches were already gone, which didn't stop Declan from milking it.

"We were trying to get you your mating gift. I got wounded!"

Alerion took Declan's hand and pressed a kiss on the back. "My poor mate! Such bravery against a skilled adversary!" The demon king winked.

Declan made a huffing sound before he grabbed Alerion's neck to pull him down for a scorching kiss. Troy, who didn't want to be left out, stepped toward them to get his own kiss.

"I was helping, too."

"And I love you for it." Alerion pulled him into his side, next to Declan. "Now explain to me why you want to get me a mating gift? I got you. That's all I ever wanted and all I'll ever need."

Troy's heart melted at those words. Their mate was so, so sweet.

"It's a werewolf tradition. We're supposed to present you with something valuable that also represents our mating."

"I understand." Alerion pressed kisses to both their foreheads. "What has the tom to do with it?" He nodded at the cat, who was back to licking his paws and looking bored.

"Well," Declan started, "you're rich. You're the demon king. Anything of material value we could give you wouldn't be too impressive, would it? And most of what we know about you is linked to the bedroom so far. This morning we saw this tom killing the biggest rat you've ever seen and just knew he'd be the perfect gift!"

"Uhm…" Alerion looked at the tom, back at Declan and Troy, then at the tom again. "I really don't want to put a damper on your obvious enthusiasm, and don't get me wrong, I love the idea of a mating gift in principle, but what made you think this...this... creature would be perfect for me? For us? Because I assume he would be living with us?"

"Can't you see it? That tom is a warrior, just like the three of us. And if we can get him to live with us, if we can catch him, you'd see what skilled hunters we are. It's perfect from every angle!" Troy grinned, his fangs showing again. He was excited like a puppy because their mate was here, they were on the hunt and they would have sex later. It didn't get much better.

Alerion rubbed small circles on Troy's nape. "Okay, I get it. Is this something you have to do alone or can I join you?"

Troy and Declan shared a look. Strictly speaking, acquiring the mating gift was their job. On the other hand, making the thrill of the hunt *part* of the gift wasn't a bad idea. Decision made, Troy smiled at their demonic lover. "You're very welcome to join us. Between the three of us, this should be a piece of cake."

\* \* \* \*

"Perhaps we should regroup and make a new plan?" Alerion had just narrowly escaped a vicious swipe of the tom's claws. Both Troy and Declan had lost some blood to the red menace, and getting the cat into their apartment by evening was looking more and more unrealistic. Troy also had the sinking feeling that the tom was toying with them. He had had numerous chances to leave the alley when they had scattered to escape the quick swipes, but he still sat in front of the dumpster, not too far from where the whole endeavor had started, looking bored whenever he wasn't trying to skin them. He probably hadn't had that much fun in ages.

"I hate to admit it, but we're no match for him. How can one cat be this quick? And he's not afraid of any of us!" Declan poked Alerion in the side.

"Isn't that the reason you chose him as my mating gift?"

"Well, yes. But a *little* fright would be good—just enough to get him into the apartment!" Declan glared at the tom. He blinked slowly, once. Clearly, he was intimidated as fuck.

"If we can't catch him with force, perhaps we can lure him with food?" At this point, Troy was willing to concede partial defeat. Getting their hands on the tom wasn't happening by force. That much was clear. Luring him into the apartment might do the trick. It wasn't a defeat per se, more a re-thinking of their strategy.

"I'll get the treats we bought!" Declan ran in the direction of their car. Troy and Alerion stayed back to eye the tom, who seemed to be mildly interested in why one third of his entertainment troupe had left.

"So, uhm, how was Budapest?"

"Exhausting." Alerion sighed. "Luckily for me, I was able to contain them before the human authorities realized there was more going on than just a huge fire in an abandoned warehouse district."

"They set a fire?" Troy knew demons were excitable and very much of the 'have fun first, think about consequences later, preferably never' persuasion, but deliberately causing a fire was over the top, even for them.

"Their line of thought was — and, yes, I'm using the term 'thought' very loosely here — that the warehouses would burn too hot for the humans to enter, so it was safe to have a friendly little squabble in there, with the added bonus of having to duck crashing rooftops and ceiling beams. Sometimes I just feel so tired."

Troy put an arm around his mate's waist. "You know what? Declan and I are going to give you a massage tonight, after we've brought your mating gift home. You can relax while we take care of everything."

Alerion rested his head on Troy's shoulder. "That sounds nice. Can we have a bath first? I love your tub."

"Of course, beloved mate. Whatever you want."

"Got it!" Declan came jogging back, holding the tube with the salmon paste high in the air. The sales lady had told them the cat who could withstand the lure of this particular treat was yet to be born.

Troy eyed the tom, who was following Declan's every movement when the man pried the cap open, got rid of the flimsy piece of aluminum serving as a seal and let the aroma of the salmon paste waft out for a moment. His wolf perked up, clearly interested. Normally fish wasn't his favorite dish — rabbit or stag were preferable — but there was something in that paste... Troy licked his lips, as did Declan and the tom.

Alerion watched them in amusement.

Very carefully, Declan squeezed some of the treat on his index finger, before he went down on one knee at a respectful distance and held it out to the tom. The cat watched him.

They watched the cat.

The tom's tail twitched. His one ear perked up.

Declan held very still, offering the fish. Troy was holding on to Alerion's arm, trying to even his breathing.

The tom got up and took a step forward.

Troy's breath caught, and he felt Alerion's muscles tensing. Declan's anticipation was like a heavy perfume in the air.

The tom took another step, causing all of them to freeze completely. He was now only a few inches from Declan's still-outstretched finger, which was trembling slightly. Whether it was from the strain of holding still or fear of losing said finger was hard to say, and Troy decided his mate was too brave to fear anything, let alone a measly red cat. Strain, it was.

The tom's neck came forward like a turtle from its shell. With a quick swipe of his tongue, he took the treat and devoured it. Still trembling — perhaps it wasn't the strain but the thrill of their hunt coming to a successful end — Declan squeezed another dollop onto his finger. The tom watched with interest as Declan pushed out his hand again.

For a moment, the tom's eyes fixated on the paste on Declan's finger, sizing it up like a mouse whose last minutes had come to pass. With bated breath, Troy and Alerion watched as the tom made the last tentative step toward Declan, its head aiming for the treat as it had done before.

The cat was so close, Troy could taste their victory on his tongue. His wolf got ready to pounce, catch the elusive feline to present it to their mate —

Things happened so fast that it took them several minutes to realize what had happened. One moment Declan was holding out his finger, waiting for the tom to come into grabbing distance, and the next he had fallen on his ass, the dollop smeared over his expensive slacks where he had tried to break his fall and not managed to get his hand to the ground fast enough and the tom was walking away with his tail held high and the entire tube in his muzzle. He jumped onto the first dumpster, looked back at them with superiority written all over his features, then proceeded to walk across the other two dumpsters where he then vanished behind them.

For a moment they stared at the now-empty alley in stunned silence. Alerion was the first to start laughing.

"I think we've just been played by a cat," he roared.

Troy looked at Declan, who had gotten back up and was rubbing his hands on his already-ruined slacks. They started laughing as well.

"Sammy always says the street cats in Beaconville are like the mafia, only meaner and more dangerous. I think he's right." Declan grinned. "The fucker knew exactly what he was doing."

"He did! Which makes him even more perfect as a mating gift. Imagine having him on our side!" Troy could already see it, them taking the tom to meetings with their most annoying business partners and letting him have at them.

"It would be brutal." Declan took both Troy's and Alerion's hand to press a kiss on each. "But I need a shower now."

"Hold your horses. I promised our poor exhausted mate a bath and a massage."

"Was it that bad?" Declan's tone was worried.

"Warehouse fire to hide the friendly fighting going on. Let's just say I don't need any barbecues in the near future." Alerion winked at them. "But I get to spend the evening being pampered by my mates, so it's not a wasted day."

"Oh, we're going to make sure of it!" Declan started dragging them in the direction of their apartment, clearly eager to start the non-violent part of their day. Troy was only too happy to follow his two mates.

# Chapter Eight

Alerion woke because he was being watched. It was a familiar feeling, honed through thousands of years of battle, where knowing an enemy was close before they could strike was the difference between victory and having to heal. His mates were restless, no doubt picking up on his unease, but they weren't fully awake yet.

They didn't need to be fearful because they had a demon to protect them. Alerion looked around the room. The door was still closed, their clothing strewn across the floor. His mates were both neat freaks, and he knew they would start picking up as soon as they got up. Pride swelled his chest. His allure was greater than the call to clean. He then checked the ceiling for any monsters that could be hanging from there, let his gaze wander from there to the door leading to the bathroom with its deliciously big tub where they had spent a great deal of the previous night, over to the walk-in closet and the dresser next to it. No signs of danger there, either. Last came the wall with the two huge windows looking out over Beaconville. The curtains on the right window weren't completely closed, and when Alerion's gaze reached the gap, he caught the glint of bright green eyes.

*The tom!*

He was sitting at the windowsill outside, watching them calmly. When he saw Alerion staring at him, he licked his muzzle.

"What's up?" Declan lifted his head, looking adorably tousled, his blond hair standing up in all directions. Troy made a sound between a growl and a groan, snuggling closer to Alerion.

"We seem to have a stalker."

That had both wolves bolting upright, low, menacing growls filling the bedroom. Alerion put a hand on each of his mates' backs, soothing them with his touch. "Over there." He pointed with his chin.

"What's he doing here?" Declan stared at the tom who hadn't moved an inch.

"Either he's staking us out or he has decided he wants more of that treat... Probably both." Troy huffed.

"Do we have more?" Alerion grabbed Declan around the waist, lifted him over his lap and onto Troy's before he started shuffling out of the bed.

"Hey! Where are you going? This could have been good!" Declan pouted.

"It's going to be better than good after we have gotten rid of our stalker — or do you want to give him a show?" Alerion winked.

He had meant it as a joke, but his wolves seemed to seriously consider the proposal — very seriously, as the sudden waft of pheromones blasting his way indicated.

"No." This was something Alerion knew he had to nip in the bud. "I'm not going to let a freaking street cat perve on me making love to my mates. No way!"

"We could just fuck like bunnies? Leave the lovemaking for later?" Troy sounded hopeful and only the twitch of his lips betrayed his teasing.

"I very much hope you know it's always making love for me, no matter how hard we fuck." Alerion was being deliberately crude, just to get another wave of those delicious pheromones. He was rewarded with not only that but also with a dual growl that hit a chord deep inside his heart.

The tom chose that moment to tap against the window.

*Not just a devious treat thief, a cockblocker as well,* Alerion thought. He hurried into the kitchen where they had left all the cat food his mates had bought for the tom. Among different cans of food and bags with kibble, he found three more tubes with the salmon paste. Grabbing one, he ran back to the bedroom where Declan had opened the curtain completely. He and Troy were having another staring match with the tom.

Alerion stepped up next to Declan and showed the tom the tube through the window. The cat perked up. He pushed his paws against the glass, yowling loud enough for all of them to hear. Declan opened the window while Alerion did the same with the tube. They all were curious what the cat would do next. If he'd come into the house, they could take that as a win...probably.

The tom turned sideways, lowered his head beneath the windowsill outside and came up with a dead rat only moments later.

Alerion stared.

When Troy and Declan had told him about the rat the tom had killed the other day, he'd thought they were joking...but no. What the tom had in his muzzle looked like a baby of one the monster rats he'd encountered in another dimension, minus the spiked tail. It was definitely too big to live in a peaceful little town like Beaconville.

Which made Alerion wonder again just what the deal was with the place.

No paranormals, except for the very select, *very powerful* group of friends his mates were part of, had claimed the town as their own.

His mates, who were uber alphas.

In a book club with a vampire of a bloodline so old that it went back to the first vampire, and a banshee who was, if Alerion wasn't completely off his game, which he never was, royalty to her people — or as close as banshees got to having royalty. They were not fond of hierarchies. Not to mention two very powerful witches and one of two real zombies in the whole world blessed by Papa Legba himself, who also *happened* to be the adopted grandson of the second real zombie who *happened* to be the witch queen of New Orleans, who *happened* to be the mate of Alerion's uncle.

Plus, Jon was mated to Barion, and Sammy, the unassuming former human and best son-in-law a demon king could wish for, who seemed to be at the center of it all, was mated to Dre.

Both of them sons of the demon king.

Who was now mated to the two uber alphas.

Those were a lot of coincidences. And if there was one unalterable law in the paranormal world, it was that there were no coincidences, which made Alerion wonder what the reason for this congregation of power was. Knowing he would find out sooner rather than later and that he most probably wouldn't like the reason, he focused back on the current situation—namely the rat dangling from the tom's mouth.

"Uh, I think he wants to make a trade." Declan stared at the feline.

"I think you're right." Alerion lifted the tube, showing it to the tom. He could practically see the complicated calculation going on behind the cat's eyes. Then he jumped inside the bedroom and dropped the rat at Alerion's feet. Both Declan and Troy wriggled their noses, and even Alerion, whose sense of smell was far worse than that of his mates, could scent the stench of the critter. But a deal had been made, and Alerion knew how to honor it. He crouched down and offered the tube to the tom.

The cat stared at him.

Then at the tube.

Then he sat down on his haunches with an air of pure arrogance. The meaning was clear. *Feed me, slave!*

Alerion sighed and squeezed a generous helping of the paste onto his finger, which he then offered to the tom like a sacrifice.

"Uhm, do you think that's a good idea?" Troy eyed the tom's muzzle. Its teeth were as sharp as its claws, no doubt. The cat cocked his head, and Alerion could have sworn he winked. Thinking over his life choices, Alerion let the scales on his hand grow out, just to be on the safe side. He had long ago outgrown his *No Risk, No Fun* phase.

The tom licked his chops when he offered him the paste again. Then he started to eat the treat from Alerion's finger with the delicacy of some purebred, prize-winning creature used to dining on the finest food from the most delicate porcelain. With a snout that had, just moments ago, carried one of the biggest rats Alerion had ever seen outside the spiked-tail rat dimension. And perhaps it was time to give all those dimensions proper names, just to spare time.

The first blob of the treat vanished quite quickly, and Alerion was reminded with a determined headbutt against his hand to keep the goodness coming. He and his mates watched in awe as the tom devoured the entire tube. When he was done, he cleaned his face with his front paw, yawned and stared at them expectantly.

"What does he want?" Alerion was puzzled. "I'm pretty sure eating the whole tube isn't too good for him. We can't give him another."

The tom kept staring.

"Perhaps there's some secret feline etiquette we aren't aware of?" Troy shrugged. He still looked half asleep and Alerion wanted nothing more than to cuddle him. Which he would have done if the tom hadn't chosen that moment to yowl. Damn beast definitely was a cockblocker.

Now the cat lowered his head to the dead rat on the floor, tapping it with its paw, looking back up at them. Alerion read pure sadism in the green gaze.

"Oh no, forget it!" He shook his head vehemently.

Troy and Declan, who seemed to have caught on to what the tom wanted, made gagging noises. The tom managed to look wounded.

Alerion immediately felt bad. The feline had come to them for an honest trade. It wasn't very grateful of them to disregard what he had to offer, was it? He looked at his mates, surprised how well their non-verbal communication was working after only a few days of being mated. Granted, some of the faces his mates were making weren't all that clear, but Alerion was a master at deduction.

*Troy: You can't be serious!*

*Declan: That thing was gods know where.*

*Alerion: It's a gift. We can't just ignore it. Look how sad he's looking.*

*Troy: I could live with that.*

*Declan: I'm not even sure this cat has feelings we can hurt.*

*Alerion: Isn't he supposed to be my mating gift? If we insult him now, he may never come back.*

*Declan: All we have to do is close the window.*

*Troy: And have a pissed-off tom in our bedroom? No, I don't think so.*

*Declan: Then what do we do?*

*Troy: Hmm…. I may have an idea.*

*Declan: I know that look.*

*Alerion: What look? What's going on?*

*Troy: Just leave it to us.*

Somehow, Troy's expression wasn't as reassuring as Alerion might have wished for. His mates started removing their sleeping clothes. Having at least pajama bottoms was one way of ensuring they got any sleep at all. He could see their muscles rippling under the skin—and not in the sexy, good times kind of way. His mates were preparing to wolf out. Alerion felt a tingle of anticipation running down his spine. He had yet to see Troy and Declan in their wolf forms. It was also a logical step to take. The wolves were probably not as picky as their human counterparts when it came to dead prey. He just hoped the tom wouldn't freak out when he suddenly shared the room with two large canines.

A quick glance confirmed that the cat was looking rather bored and not at all amused that they were dragging their feet on accepting the prey he had offered so generously—well, in exchange for a sugared-up treat he probably shouldn't have in the first place, but that was semantics. Magic rushed through the room and encased his two mates to turn them into their wolfish counterparts. Alerion had seen countless shifters change their forms, and he was proud at how smoothly his mates did it. There was no horrific breaking of bones or pained grunting, not even a sigh. One moment there were two very naked, very delicious men standing in front of the bed, the next, two wolves occupied their place.

Two very large wolves.

Practically horses.

If horses had fangs almost as long as Alerion's forearm... Uber alphas were indeed a class of their own. Luckily, his mates retained their hair color in their shifted forms, making them easy to distinguish. Declan's coat was a mixture of different shades of blond, coming together harmoniously, while Troy showed the same gorgeous dark brown with hints of golden-red as his human form. Both coats were shining and meticulously groomed, which didn't surprise Alerion. In fact, he was looking forward to endless hours of combing the silky fur and felt a little sad that all his scales needed from time to time was a little oil. Then again, applying oil could be fun as well.

The two wolves posed for Alerion, showing off their huge bodies to him. After he had praised them for their strong, sleek forms and gorgeous fur, they turned toward the tom.

Who was licking his ass...again.

When Troy growled at him, he looked up and hissed in warning, his only ear flat on his head. It was clear the tom wasn't acting out of fear, just showing his annoyance. Troy made a rumbling sound that seemed to mollify the feline, because the tom's ear pricked up again. He cocked his head, scrutinizing both wolves with a calculating gleam in his eyes. Then he pushed the dead rat toward them.

Declan lowered his head to sniff the creature before he gave an appreciative rumble. The tom puffed up visibly. He apparently wasn't as aloof as he had made them think. Fascinated, Alerion watched as the three predators conducted some kind of conversation with the dead rat as the main topic. It consisted mostly of growls and hisses, some determined nudging of the critter's lifeless form and a fluffing up of fur.

All of a sudden, the tom's right front paw flipped forward, launching the rat into the air. Declan immediately jumped after it, catching it in his muzzle at the highest point of its flight curve and sending it flying across the room with one swing of his head. Troy followed, his powerful hindlegs propelling him across their bed and back down to the ground only inches before he would have crashed against the wall. Meanwhile the tom had flitted under the bed, no doubt to get to the rat as well, as the menacing growl from Troy suggested. When the dead critter came flying back in his direction, minus some fur, Alerion had had enough. As much as he didn't want the tom to be sad that they didn't appreciate his gift, he drew the line at having bits of rat all over their bedroom.

"Stop it!" He put all his authority behind those two words and, miracle of miracles, it worked. His two wolf mates slinked back to him, whining a bit and rubbing against his legs to apologize. The tom came to him as well, not whining but definitely looking chagrined.

"I know you just want to have some fun, and I'm well aware that your predatory nature makes it easy for you to play with something dead, but this is our bedroom. You can play someplace else with one of the rubber toys you bought." He was mainly talking to Declan and Troy, but the tom seemed to understand him as well. His tail twitched, then he yowled and nudged Declan's hind leg with his head.

Both Declan and Troy started wagging their tails before they bounded off in the direction of the kitchen where the various cat toys were stashed. The tom followed quickly, not even sparing Alerion a glance.

*So much for this being my mating gift*, he thought, amused.

There was a crash from the kitchen, followed by howling and hissing, then another crash and a triumphant yowl. The short yips coming from his mates told Alerion they had accepted whatever challenge had been issued. He sighed and shifted his hand to grab the rat with the tips of his claws, careful to not slice it in half. It was going to be a long day.

He smiled.

A long day with his mates and his mating gift, full of love and ridiculousness and silliness, and he knew he wouldn't want it any other way.

# Chapter Nine

It was the second day after they had caught the still nameless tom — Declan would stick with this story, no matter what — and he and Troy were at Sammy's bookstore to get their caffeine fix for the afternoon. After a tiresome video call with one of their companies in Canada, they had decided to take a break before they tackled all the paperwork their four PAs had sent them. At least they would be working from home, with their new addition to the family warming their feet — ha, more likely chewing off their toes, but who cared about such insignificant details? — while they waited for Alerion to come back from Iceland where a bunch of demons had apparently decided to play trolls for the natives. If his mate hadn't been so stressed out, Declan was sure he would have seen the ingenuity of his subjects as a positive.

Declan watched as Sammy made their coffee, his movements like a poem of grace and efficiency while Troy tried to decide which baked goods they would be taking with them. Dre was sprawled on one of the sofas, reading *Alice's Adventures in Wonderland*, the next book they would be discussing at the book club.

Milo was at the back of the store where Declan could hear him silently cursing while he unpacked the latest shipment of antique books. Sammy had not-so-stealthily started teaching the young man the finer aspects of book dealership to have a reason to pay him a higher wage. Despite Milo also working for Quirion and earning quite the check for his troubles, he was still in a bit of a pinch regarding his plans for going to MIT. He would most definitely get a scholarship, his grades were straight As throughout and he was studying like mad for the admission exam, but living costs weren't covered, and even though Milo's mom was doing well, she still had her scheduled operation and needed regular visits with the doctors because of her breast cancer diagnosis. Of course, nobody in their group would let her die if money got too tight, but they all respected Milo's wish to make it on his own. If there was some discreet help in the form of bonus checks, nobody said a word about it.

"Here you are." Sammy put the two travel mugs with caffeinated goodness on the counter. "You really need to get Dad one of these as well. Then I can make him his hot chocolate."

Declan stared at Sammy, wondering how such a genius could be hiding in this small body. From the corner of his eye, he saw Troy already typing on his phone, no doubt ordering their mate his very own eco-friendly bamboo travel mug.

"Have you decided on your pastries yet? Or do you want one of each? They've made the raspberry vanilla muffins today, if you haven't seen." Sammy gestured toward one of the glass domes to his right. Declan immediately reached for it to confirm that there were indeed three of the delicious muffins left. Three muffins for three mates. *Perfect.* He nodded for Sammy to pack them up, together with the cookies Troy had selected. He was just reaching for his wallet when the door chime announced a visitor.

No…visitors. Declan stiffened when the sweet scent of two omegas assaulted his nostrils.

"Fuck," Troy muttered under his breath.

"What is it?" Sammy looked at them with confusion written all over his face. He was very good at reading the mood in a room, and he had surely picked up on their sudden tension.

"Are you the uber alphas?" a timid-sounding voice asked.

Sammy made a squawking sound, which had Dre rushing to his side.

Declan turned toward the newcomers in sync with Troy. They were young, not older than early twenties, too young to approach two uber alphas all on their own—and on their own they were. Declan sniffed and could sense no other shifters close by.

"Who are you?" he asked, his annoyance bleeding through, which caused both omegas to lower their gazes. He cursed inwardly, a colorful string of expletives he had collected over the years, some in different languages, before he took a deep breath. Troy was doing a similar breathing exercise next to him, no doubt picking up on his agitation and feeding it with his own. This whole situation had 'council' and 'clusterfuck' written all over it.

"I'm sorry. I didn't mean to be harsh," Declan started in a much softer tone while picturing Elder Simarl drenched in honey and thrown into a pit with hungry ants. It soothed him enough to keep his agitation down. "Who are you?" He repeated his question from before, in case the two omegas were too terrified to remember it.

They both lifted their heads, and the one with the mop of black curls started to speak. "I'm Tino, and this is Jules." He gestured to the other omega, who had long red hair down to his waist, which was an uncommon color among wolves. Depending on how old-fashioned his pack was, this could either be a reason to make him the very lowest on the totem pole or it was seen as a uniqueness that could garner him some advantages. Just looking at the omega made it hard to tell, though something in Declan's gut told him it was the second. Advantage or not, it hadn't spared him from having to come here and face the uber alphas, though.

Both men were petite, even for omegas. Their features had a certain feminine quality Declan didn't miss. Apparently Elder Simarl and the rest of the council thought they could somehow sway them with two admittedly very pretty faces.

Pretty faces with tears streaming down from huge eyes. Tino's were of a light amber, while Jules' were seafoam green. Both wore thin cotton T-shirts, which were snug enough to leave little to the imagination. Their jeans were practically painted on, hugging their asses. Declan had to give it to the council, though. They had tried for some variety, apart from hair color.

Tino was a bit rounder than Jules and had more curves to his frame, while Jules was mainly thin. Both their forearms had definition—not a surprise, because it was impossible for a werewolf not to gain some muscle mass from just breathing. All in all, the two omegas looked like the perfect bait for any horny alpha looking for a good time. Add in the tears brimming in their eyes and even Declan's wolf, who usually had zero interest in omegas, felt the need to protect them.

Next to him, Troy took a deep breath. "You're drenched in pheromones. Let me guess... The council sends you with best regards?"

*Or* the omegas were using substances to trick the two uber alphas into a reaction. Declan felt his irritation rise.

"Why would you perfume yourself with pheromones?" Sammy asked from behind the counter. Dre was looming over him like a particularly scary shadow. He would have been more intimidating if he weren't trying to hide a laugh. *The bastard.*

"They've done it or were told to do it in the hopes to trigger our wolves into mating with them." Troy's voice was matter-of-fact, not betraying the absolute rage bleeding through their bond.

"But you can't! You're already mated to Dad!" Sammy was clearly torn between pity for the two cowering omegas and righteous outrage on behalf of his father-in-law. Well, father, because that's what Alerion was to Sammy.

"Yes, we are, which means those pheromones aren't working—at least not on us." Declan looked at the two omegas. "It's very dangerous, going around smelling like that. What if you attracted unwanted attention?"

Tino's eyes went wide. "They said there was only you here. No other shifters," he whispered. "We only applied it when we knew where the store was. We didn't walk far like this."

"Well, at least you've got some sense." Declan sighed. "We can't give you what you want, though.

You heard Sammy. We're mated. There is no other for us."

The tears in both omegas' eyes started flowing over again. "But you have to!" Tino wailed. "The council — "

"The council is a bunch of assholes who can fuck themselves, as far as we are concerned." Troy said, his tone much kinder than his words.

For a moment, both Tino and Jules just stared at them. Then the tears started in earnest, dripping down on their thin T-shirts in a steady stream. Their shoulders trembled like leaves in a summer storm.

"Do something!" Sammy looked at them over the counter. "These poor guys!"

Declan looked at Troy, who sighed. There was only one thing they could do. They stepped toward the omegas. Troy hugged Tino while Declan pulled Jules into his arms. As much as it galled him, the best way to soothe an agitated werewolf, especially an omega, was to snuggle. Not when they were fully wolved out, obviously, but in all other cases, it worked. The sobs coming from Jules were already decreasing. Tino, too, seemed to calm down — which, of course, was the exact moment Alerion appeared in the bookshop.

"Uhm, what's going on here?"

Declan had to admit their mate was a lot calmer than they would have been had the roles been reversed. Had to be the extra centuries Alerion had on them. With age came wisdom and patience and so on.

Before he could start explaining to his mate, Dre opened his mouth, trying to make everything worse. "Well, these two delicious omegas were apparently sent by the council as some kind of gift for Troy and Declan. They were dunked in werewolf pheromones to make your mates do something irreversible, like take them right here in Sammy's shop, marring Sammy and me for life in the process and produce little uber werewolf pups for the council and their plans of world dominion. Did I forget anything?"

"No, I think that's it. Though I didn't know werewolf males could have babies! Oh, and I thought there could only ever be one uber werewolf walking the earth? Two, if they are mates?" The gleam in Sammy's eyes told Declan they would be in for a long session of question and answer about werewolf reproduction once this mess was sorted. He wondered what bribe it would take for Mavis and Maribel to explain the werewolf bees to Sammy?

Declan looked at Alerion, who cocked his head. "Why are you hugging them? Are those pheromones working?" He sniffed the air. "It does smell a bit sweet in here. I thought it was the pastries."

"Most of it is. It's quite subtle, even for our noses." Declan pointed at the omega in his arms. "By the way, this is Jules and this" —he nodded toward Troy—"is Tino. We're snuggling them because they are highly agitated, and werewolves calm down more easily when they have skin contact."

Alerion nodded. "I thought as much. Tino, Jules, are you here on the council's orders?" he asked softly.

Declan felt Jules shuddering in his arms. "We're not supposed to tell, but you know already, and it's wrong to lie to the uber alphas. Elder Simarl and the others sent us to sleep with the uber alphas and have their offspring."

"You're not even in heat. How did they think this would go?" Alerion still sounded so collected.

"They-they said instinct would take over." Tino sniffled. "And-and we would go into heat once we had-

had sex and..." He shuddered violently. Clearly, his willingness to be mounted by an alpha crazed out by pheromones was beyond zero.

Unfortunately, as Declan was well aware, omegas didn't have much choice when it came to orders from alphas — or really any shifter higher in the hierarchy. It was another reason they had turned their backs on their fellow shifters, though he was starting to think that might have been a mistake. Tino and Jules wouldn't have to be here if Troy and Declan had changed a few things in shifter society. Then again, if they hadn't turned their backs on it all, they probably wouldn't have met Alerion. Declan sighed inwardly. This was the kind of thinking that bred migraines more quickly than one could say the word 'complicated'.

"Why don't you two lie down in my apartment and get some rest before we keep talking about this?" Sammy had rounded the counter and was placing a hand on each of the omegas' backs. "You can also take a shower, and Dre will get you some fresh clothes. How does that sound?"

"But the council..." Tino trailed off. He was clearly relieved to not have to go through with this harebrained scheme.

"I don't think the council expects you to be pregnant right away. And if so, they are even bigger morons than I thought." Declan looked first at Alerion, then to Troy, who both nodded. Once Tino and Jules had calmed down, they would talk to them in detail before they decided what to do about the council.

This confrontation had always been inevitable, and Declan would have preferred it if the old farts had taken their time going after them. Then again, dealing with them now meant they didn't have to do it in the future. Making things clear once and for all was for the best.

He slowly stepped back from Jules, who seemed to have calmed down enough to let go of him. Troy was doing the same.

"Hi, I'm Sammy. This is my book shop, and I'd be happy if you stayed with me until we get this mess sorted." Dre's mate took both omegas' hands, tugging them toward the side entrance of the shop, which led to his and Dre's apartment. "Did you know my mate can slice space and time? Have you ever traveled that way? It's so amazing. Oooh, I know! Dre, beloved, why don't you magic us up? Milo? Can you hold the fort for a while?" Sammy was in full mother-hen mode now. From the back of the shop came a muffled "No problem", followed by a rumbling sound and some choice curse words Declan would swear Milo hadn't learned from him and Troy. The boy was much too young for such filthy language. *Quirion.*

Dre winked at them before he approached Sammy and his charges with a friendly smile. To their credit, the two omegas didn't flinch, even though they were immune to the glamour that made Dre look like a very hunky, but also very human man to other humans. Instead, they saw him in his full non-shifted glory, red skin and all. Luckily, he had his wings tucked in and his claws sheathed. "It's just a short ride, but I hope you'll enjoy it." He grew out one of his claws and sliced space and time. A moment later, he, Sammy and the two omegas were gone, the only proof of them having been there the faint smell of pheromones in the air.

"Do I get my welcome home kisses now?" Alerion winked at them. The shop was still empty, no human customers they could offend with a little PDA. Declan stepped forward at the same time as Troy, joining him in a three-way kiss. They were getting better at it, thanks to hours and hours of practice. After they broke apart because Milo cleared his throat none too subtly, Declan had time to look at his mate properly. Alerion looked exhausted.

"Dare I ask how Iceland was?"

Alerion shook his head. "It's a gorgeous island, and we definitely have to go there sometime when I don't have to herd demons. We're just lucky Icelanders are more open when it comes to the paranormal, because my subjects had already managed to get mentioned in the newspaper."

"What did you do?" Troy was rubbing soothing circles on their mate's back while Declan did the same to Alerion's front.

"I told them Iceland was off limits for the time being. I didn't have to glamour anybody, because the people who had seen them were convinced they were trolls, which fits with their set of beliefs. No harm done, at least not as much as there could have been. There's little chance the story will make it out of Iceland, and even if it does, it will be reported as part of the oddities Icelanders display."

"Hmm. If Iceland is more open, why not tell your demons they have to go there to play?" Declan nuzzled Alerion's clavicles.

"Uhm, I love you, Declan, you know I do, but are you listening to yourself? Telling *our* demons they are allowed to go someplace and have fun? That's like giving a kid the keys to the candy store. You won't recognize it once they're done."

"I guess you're right. I hadn't thought that one through." Declan peppered some kisses on Alerion's chest.

"You'll get used to it. You have eternity to learn."

Declan shuddered. Said like that, eternity lost some of its appeal.

"How about we go home and have a nice long bubble bath?" Troy chimed in. "Let's not think about future problems but the pleasures to be had now."

"You're such a wise man at your young age." Alerion kissed first Troy, then Declan. "Yes, let's go home. I thought you had work, though?"

"Just boring paperwork we can do later as well." Declan wove his fingers with Alerion's and Troy's.

"Let's get our coffee and pastries and go." Troy pulled in the direction of the counter to get their stuff.

Alerion was getting ready to slice space and time to take them home when another rip in the fabric of reality appeared, letting through a pink demon Declan recognized as one of Alerion's PAs.

"Eliam, what are you doing here?" Alerion's wary tone made Declan antsy.

The pink demon bowed deeply. "My king. I'm so sorry to disturb you, but I have…worrying news."

# Chapter Ten

"They did *what*?"

Troy felt pity for the poor demon who had popped in with the news that a group of demons were currently at a renaissance fair somewhere in Bavaria to 'have fun'. Demons having fun usually meant everybody else was suffering. Putting an end to this little excursion sadly took precedence over their plans with the bubble bath and the tub. Their gorgeous demon mate was already preparing to slice time and space, and Declan and Troy were quick to step next to him. Alerion nodded gratefully. Anger and exhaustion were warring on his face, making Troy vow to find a solution to get their mate his much-needed downtime.

They stepped through the rift and right into the past, as it seemed. Alerion had opened the gate between some trees to hide their sudden appearance. Even a demon's glamour couldn't overcome the very solid proof of three men stepping out of nowhere, but he needn't have bothered. The fair, it appeared, was in full swing. The sun was low on the horizon, preparing to go down, leaving behind a sweltering heat Troy wouldn't have associated with Bavaria.

All over the field in front of them, fires were lit in between tents from different times in human history. Troy never paid too much attention when Sammy and Dre started nerding about history, but even he recognized some of the periods — Viking, Germanic, Celtic, early Medieval. People in stunningly beautiful costumes — Troy would have loved to know if they were accurate as well but assumed that was the case the whole place just had this kind of vibe — were going about their business, though not nearly enough to fill all the tents. After a quick glance around, they spotted an arena built from wood behind the expanse of tents. A definitely non-human roar coming from that direction jerked them into running at full speed, dodging tents and humans on their way to where the wayward demons *had* to be.

Several possible scenarios were running through Troy's mind, none of them good. They all involved copious amounts of blood. Their poor mate would probably have to glamour everybody on site.

Around the arena was a wooden fence with gates they could have easily jumped over. The gates were in line with the entrances to the arena, providing a direct path. Each gate was guarded by a human, all in costume. They came to a halt in front of a Viking warrior. She had her long blonde hair shaved at the sides, her tribal tattoos framed by the long, thin braids she had bound to a messy ponytail on top of her head. Her leather and fur armor was inlaid with even more tribal patterns, and her sword looked very real. One discreet sniff confirmed it was definitely made of metal, and Troy hoped it wasn't sharpened. Wasn't that forbidden at these fairs? He didn't know and didn't want to find out the painful way. Being in close proximity to a potentially dangerous weapon put his wolf even more on edge than it already had been. Troy had to concentrate not to sprout fur.

The woman held up her hand. "Tickets?"

They stared at her. "Tickets?" Alerion parroted.

She nodded. "We've got this super-cool group of demon warriors doing a demonstration tonight. The arena was sold out within minutes. Man, the costumes on these guys…"

Troy was glad that Alerion's magic allowed them to understand the string of fast-paced German the woman was spouting with a smiling face, not knowing she was causing Alerion a minor heart attack.

"*Demonstration?*" he croaked.

"Yes. It's of the fantasy type, obviously, with them being demons and all, but a pinch of *World of Warcraft* has never harmed anybody, don't you agree?"

Alerion clearly begged to differ. "You're telling me a bunch of *my* demons are in there, giving a…a *demonstration* of demonic warfare?" Alerions scales were starting to show. Declan and Troy moved closer, touching their mate to calm him down. The woman was thankfully oblivious to the scales rippling over Alerion's skin, as well as his clearly agitated state.

"Yeah, that's so cool." She blinked at them, and for a moment, Troy worried she had picked up on something. Once a human shed their protective blindness, they became hyperaware of everything paranormal and were notoriously hard to put back into a state of ignorant bliss—case in point Sammy, who, once he had awoken to the other world surrounding him, had turned into some kind of magnet for paranormal creatures and activity.

He needn't have worried. The woman had picked up on something, though not what he had feared. "You said '*my* demons'. Are you their trainer? That would be so cool. I can't tell you how much I admire their form!"

Troy realized this was their chance to get inside the arena without those pesky tickets they didn't have anyhow. He nodded.

"Yes, he is. We're his assistants. We had a delay coming here, but it's important for the troupe's morale to see their trainer." He was laying it on a bit thick, and it worked. The woman smirked sympathetically.

"I know. Traffic is a bitch on weekends, especially in this area. Everybody needs to be somewhere." She sighed and started opening the gate. "Come in. The demonstration has already started."

They hurried past her, throwing out a 'Thank you'. Led by the noise, they found their way to the backstage area, where they immediately spotted three demons. It wasn't hard. They were partly shifted, their scales gleaming in the sinking sun, their forms towering over the few humans around them. The weapons they had casually resting against their thighs and across their shoulders — a bihänder with a serrated blade, a battle axe made from blue metal most certainly not found on Earth and a warhammer the dwarfs in *Lord of the Rings* would have been proud of, though they wouldn't have been able to lift it, because the head was roughly the size of a Shetland pony and probably the same weight — were most definitely sharpened, as were their claws, which were on full display. One of the biggest no-nos for paranormals was showing their assets, and these demons were just carelessly flaunting them in everybody's faces.

Alerion growled low, and the two demons and one demoness turned toward the sound. When they saw him, they started to smile.

One important thing Troy had learned over the course of the last week, was that a demon's concept of guilt was even vaguer than their concept of responsibility. If Alerion told them not to, say, set a warehouse district on fire to have a little fight in it, they wouldn't do it anymore—which wouldn't stop them from setting fire to an abandoned factory to have a friendly scuffle, because clearly, that wasn't a warehouse. Dealing with demons was so exhausting because they were so damn good at finding loopholes, hence the absolute absence of guilt and genuine joy of seeing their king. They had nothing to fear because clearly, they hadn't done anything forbidden. It was demon psychology 101.

"My king." The demoness stepped forward. She bore the bronze markings of a demon warrior, while the two males showed the black tattoos of normal demons.

"Allienna, who are your friends?" The question in itself was strange, because demons usually didn't have demon friends—at least not for long until a fight broke out. The fact that more than these three demons were here was highly alarming.

The demoness gestured for her companions to come forward. They both bowed their heads. "Dioran and Serpamon, my king. Are you here to watch the show? That would be such an honor!"

Troy could see Alerion was doing his best not to shout at his subjects. Declan was busy scanning the backstage area for potential threats, his wolf as on edge as Troy's.

"What exactly does this…'show' entail?" Alerion sounded like a man who knew asking that question would make him unhappy but did it anyway, because there was no way around it.

Allienna clapped her hands in obvious delight about the interest her king was showing. "First, there are the duels. We have six pairs who fight each other until a winner is determined. That's what's going on at the moment." She waved her battle axe in the direction where Troy thought the fighting ring was. They could hear the banging of metal, some heavy grunting and other sounds of serious fighting, overlayed by the cheers of the audience and the troubling swish of the axe cutting through air. Just thinking about it making contact with fragile human skin and bones had Troy shuddering. This was a disaster in the making if he'd ever seen one.

"Then we do a battle situation, ten against ten, to make things more interesting. They're getting ready for it over there." The battle axe swung to the right, where Troy thought he could see flashes of steel and scales.

Declan groaned, expressing Troy's thoughts perfectly. So far, they had counted thirty-five demons, which was far from the allowed ten demons per gathering. Allienna seemed to have realized this as well, because she lifted the axe in what was meant to be placating gesture. "I know, that's more than the allowed number for a *gathering*, but we keep separated. Six pairs out in the arena, we three here, the demons preparing for the battle have split into two groups as well. No more than ten. And once the battle starts, we'll spread out, everybody sticking to their assigned group or the opponent they're fighting." She smiled, showing her sharp teeth, so happy she was obeying the rules.

Alerion rubbed his face with his hands. "And after the battle?"

Allienna beamed. "That's the best part. We're giving instructions, showing the humans how to improve their fighting. Some of them are really talented."

Troy heard Declan coughing and hurried to put a placating hand on Alerion's back.

"You give the humans fighting lessons?" Alerion's voice was strangely weak, as if he had finally cracked under the strain.

It was a rather interesting idea, Troy had to admit. Until now, humans and other non-demonic beings had been more of a collateral damage when demons had their fun — except for the really bad demons, who were all locked away by now. Teaching them to fight showed the intent of active inclusion, which was never a good idea when it came to demons. With them, the strictest segregation was the way to go.

"Oooh, yes. They love it. And afterward, we get beer and human food roasted over the fire…and money. They *pay* for it!" Allienna was clearly mystified as to why somebody would pay to be taught to be a better fighter. For demons, it was part of their upbringing, just like learning the demonic language or how to hop through space and time.

"You do demonstrations of demonic warfare at renaissance fairs and get paid to teach fighting skills. How long has this been going on?" Alerion didn't seem to have any fight left in him. Troy snuggled up against him to lend some of his strength. He could see why nobody ever challenged Alerion for the position of king. Only an idiot would want to herd such a bag of fleas.

"Uhm, guys, how long have we been doing this?" Allienna turned to the two demons who twirled their weapons, deep in thought.

"I think this is our tenth fair…or the twelfth?" Serpamon lifted his bihänder, contemplating the elaborate etchings along the blade.

Allienna shrugged. "Ten or twelve, doesn't matter. It's going *great!*" She beamed at Alerion. "And we're honored you brought your mates with you!" She bowed in Declan's and Troy's direction. It was kind of a late acknowledgement, though not unusual or meant in a belittling manner, as Troy knew. Demons just didn't put that much stock in hierarchies. They saw them more as friendly suggestions — with the exception of the king, of course.

"Uhm, it's an honor to meet you, Allienna." Declan glanced at Alerion, whose jaw was working as if he were chewing a particularly sinewy piece of meat. All of a sudden, Troy found the situation with the council and the two omegas positively harmless. At least Tino and Jules hadn't come wielding huge weapons threatening to kill humans and expose their entire species to the non-paranormal world. Small blessings and all that.

"I'm not sure I can let this go on, Allienna," Alerion began. The demoness's shoulders slumped.

"Why not? We're being super-careful, my King. The humans think this is a show! We're not hurting anybody." She hesitated for a moment, clearly not wanting to lie to her sovereign. "No humans, anyway. Demons heal." The petulant tone reminded Troy of

Amber when she tried to understand something everybody else thought was obvious.

Alerion sighed. He opened his mouth, no doubt to start a long-winded explanation why it was indeed a very bad idea to mix humans and demons, no matter why or how, but Declan was faster.

"Perhaps we should see what exactly they are doing, my beloved mate? At the moment, it seems to me that ending the show would garner more attention than just letting it run its course." He looked at Troy, silently asking for his opinion.

"Declan isn't wrong, Alerion. And we're here now." He didn't say *'what can go wrong?'* because that was a sure-fire method to jinx them all. Judging by the dark look Alerion was shooting him, he had sensed the direction of Troy's thoughts.

"Fine. I'm going to watch your show to determine— I don't know what there is to determine, but I will do it."

"Wonderful!" Allienna clapped her hands, immune to the vagueness of her king's words. As far as she was concerned, her day couldn't go any better, judging by the way she was bouncing on her toes while happily swinging the axe through the air. The gentle *woosh* reminded Troy of a ceiling fan working overtime. Only ceiling fans couldn't decapitate a person in one ugly go.

"Uhm, you might want to put that down."

"Ups. Sorry. I'm just so happy!" Allienna let the axe dangle at her side. "Please, my King, follow me. There's a spot right at the entrance to the arena where you'll be able to see everything. You, too, of course." She motioned for Declan and Troy to follow as well. "Dioram, tell the others our king and his mates are here. I'm sure they want to impress them with their fighting prowess."

While Allienna ushered them toward the entrance to the arena, where the clanging of metal and the grunts of pain were getting louder and louder, Troy shuddered, thinking of already over-enthusiastic demons trying to impress Alerion. It was like adding Mentos to a bottle of Cola — only to be attempted under strictly supervised circumstances.

Even if loosely interpreted, an arena full of humans didn't fall under the definition of 'strictly supervised'. It was more a case of let's see what Ragnarök *could* look like if the Nordic gods put a little effort in.

They stepped next to their mate at the gate, looking out into the arena, where indeed demons were fighting. There were only two pairs left. The other four were standing at the sidelines, either banging their weapons against the wooden planks or groaning and trying to stay upright, depending on the severity of their wounds. Even knowing demons healed quickly, Troy felt a little sick when he saw the twisted wrist of the one standing closest to them. He didn't seem to mind too much, and strangely enough, the humans didn't either. Their focus was on the remaining fighters, mostly.

"Is this glamour?" Troy asked Alerion, staring at the demon whose wrist was slowly twisting back to the right setting.

His mate furrowed his brows. "Partly. The rest is blissful ignorance and the firm belief in extremely advanced technology making all this possible." He groaned softly. "I think I'm getting a migraine."

"I don't think demons can get one of those. Look... We have a winner." Declan gestured at the arena, where a silver-colored demon was raising her arms high in the air, clutching the shaft of a double-axe with bronze inlays. The crowd went wild, whooping and cheering while the loser limped toward the entrance to the arena, leaving a trail of greenish blood on the ground. When the demon reached them, the source of the blood, a deep gash on his thigh, had already closed. He smiled happily at them.

"My King, esteemed mates! Such an honor to have you here!"

"Uh, yes, you do know you've been bleeding all over the place?" Troy pointed at the green puddles on the ground.

"Yeah, Le'anna got me good there." The demon didn't seem to see any problem. Troy thought he felt a throbbing between his temples. Maybe paranormals had a hard time getting a migraine, but it was definitely possible. He couldn't imagine how his poor mate dealt with it all on a daily basis.

"Uhm, demon blood…on the ground of an arena filled with humans." Hopefully, Troy watched for signs of — he didn't know — insight, perhaps?

"That actually works in our favor, Mate of my King," Allienna chimed in. "The humans think this is a show, and it's even more realistic because the spilled fluids are not red."

"First of all, call me Troy. And this is Declan." He nodded toward his other mate. "Secondly, are you sure?"

"Oh yes. I overheard some of them talking after our last show. They thought it was a nice touch, "*a well-thought-out detail*," they said." Allienna was back to happily swinging her axe around again. "We're doing great!"

Troy looked at Alerion. The demons might be doing great, but his poor mate looked ready for a thousand years of holiday.

# Chapter Eleven

The problem was, Alerion decided, that he could actually see the logic. If his demons were just plain ignorant, trying to cause him trouble on purpose, he could have gone into a rage and perhaps roughed up some of them, just to get his point across. As it was, he couldn't argue with what they were saying. Not much, anyway. Iceland had shown him that humans could be even more gullible than he ever thought possible. The problem was, there were always some who saw more than they should. It was a concept his demons didn't understand.

Allienna was now marching into the arena, congratulating Le'anna, who bowed to the audience one last time before she jogged in their direction. Allienna announced the start of the group combat to the joyful whistling and cheering of the crowd, telling an elaborate story about why the two groups were fighting.

Alerion smiled, despite the worries nagging at him. His subjects were actually having fun with humans involved, and so far, none of them had come to harm. A tiny flicker of hope woke in his chest that perhaps evolution was possible, even for demons.

He heard stomping and turned around to see the two demon groups that had prepared for the battle demonstration lining up to enter the arena. Allienna shouted something, the cheering increased in volume and the first ten demons ran onto the field with a lot more discipline than the regular demon scuffle saw. Usually there was no discernible formation because nobody could expect a bunch of individual fighters to do something as tiresome as sync with their fellow fighters, which was demon warfare in a nutshell, or so Alerion's experience went.

When the second group trooped into the arena and Allienna started the fighting by swinging her axe above her head in a wide circle before she leisurely strolled back to them, casually ducking flying spears and some knives on the way, Alerion had to admit that his demons were good. What they were showing was, of course, not real demon warfare, because then all the spectators would be dead already and the fight would have expanded to the entire area, but what humans probably thought was how creatures from hell—their interpretation, not his—solved their conflicts. There was a lot of shouting and screaming involved, sharp weapons bouncing back harmlessly from thick demonic scales, happy chuckles, the familiar sound of bones breaking and, above it all, the roaring of the crowd.

"That's not how demons fight." He looked at Allienna, who was now standing next to him and his mates, watching the proceedings like a hawk.

"I know. It took some getting used to, but actually, it's more fun like this. I never realized a fight could be about more than just the glory of bathing in your enemies' blood." Her fangs elongated a bit while she said this, her scales rippling over her skin.

"Oh," Alerion said weakly. He felt both his mates' hands on his back, which reminded him he was no longer alone in the madness. Though this was an entirely new kind of madness he wasn't sure what to make of.

"Yes," Allienna went on, oblivious to his weak response. "The applause and cheering are exhilarating. We love it." And that was definitely progress.

"Your fighting choreography is pretty impressive. Did you come up with all of this on your own?" Troy's gaze was riveted on the combatants, who were clashing happily again and again.

"Some of it we came up with on our own, some we copied from human movies. I never knew they weren't real, you know. What a surprise, and our main source, was, of course, *Demon Wars*."

Alerion choked on air. Next to him, Troy and Declan coughed loudly. "You know about *Demon Wars*?"

Allienna beamed. "Oh yes. Your son and his esteemed mate are so ingenious. It's thanks to them and their demo releases that we can come up with all these great ideas for new challenges."

It took a moment for the words to filter through Alerion's befuddled brain. He blamed the battle cries of the demons in the arena. Declan, on the other hand, was quick on the uptake.

"You mean, all those incidents in the past months? You were re-enacting different levels from Barion's and Jon's video game?"

Allienna's smile was now so wide that there was no hiding the sharpness of all her teeth. "Yes. I admit it's sometimes hard to find a fitting location, because the levels don't come with maps, but that's part of the fun as well."

Troy turned to Alerion. "I thought *Demon Wars* was modelled after the actual demon wars? Why wouldn't they recognize the places those battles have taken place?"

Alerion sighed. His problem with his demons doing reckless things all over the planet had just gained another facet, making everything more complicated, because now his family was directly involved. How should he break it to Jon and Barion, that their precious video game had to vanish from the market?

"Well, not all demons took part in all demon wars. Some were born later, some, not many, are dead—and don't forget a demon's tendency to forget details. All most of them remember about even the battles they were involved in is the wounds they inflicted. The only reason Barion and Jon can come up with such accurate descriptions is because of Barion's gift. Plus, they're mixing up places and battles, which makes it even harder to recognize them."

"Oh, I hadn't thought of that." Troy patted his back. "On the upside, things seem to be a little less violent?" His tone made clear he was grasping for straws. Declan and Troy might not have been his mates for long—almost two weeks hardly counted—but even they knew that even if things were less violent now, it didn't mean they would stay that way. Any moment one of his demons could get overexcited and *bam*, instant bloodbath among innocent humans. Another cheer from the crowd had him looking at the arena again where two demons were rounding on a third, literally ramming him into the ground. *Well*, he thought, *innocent for a given value of it.* Not like Sammy, who truly had a heart made of the softest cotton and also one that was a lot bigger on the inside.

Still pondering how he should deal with this situation, Alerion watched as one group of demons defeated the other and the humans went crazy for the 'show'.

After that, the demons started with the lessons. Allienna had a huge metal helmet with two impressive horns Alerion was sure had come from a living creature not at home on Earth, where everybody who was interested in getting some practical tips could drop the number of their ticket for the show.

Dioram drew the lucky winners, who came down into the arena to get their instructions. This was the part Alerion would have been tempted to stop, but again, his mates reminded him how that would draw more attention than letting things run their course. He had to trust Allienna and her assurances of how often they had already pulled this off without a hitch. Watching how careful all the demons were not to hurt the humans they were paired with, Alerion had to admit things weren't as bad as he had feared.

He must have drifted off a bit, leaning into the touches of his mates on his back and arms, enjoying their soft ministrations, because he was caught completely off guard when he heard his name announced loudly by Allienna.

"Alerion, our king!"

Troy and Declan must have been in the same trance as he, because they, too, startled. Allienna waved at him to step into the arena. People were clapping like mad. Still befuddled, Alerion walked toward her into the brightly lit oval where demonic blood had soaked into the sawdust, making it look a bit like a perverse rainbow. He bowed to the crowd, accepting their cheers, even though he wasn't sure what they were for. Demons didn't cheer each other.

"My king, I'm sure the audience would be delighted if you could share some of your wisdom with them. After all, you are one of our most supreme fighters!"

And he was back to getting a migraine. No way would he take part in this madness, teaching a naturally violent species how to be even more destructive and—He hesitated. There was one thing he could teach them, something good and wholesome. Alerion took over from Allienna, smiling at the crowd.

"Thank you so much for your hospitality. I think we've had enough fighting for one evening."

There were some boos, and Alerion hurried on.

"You know what always comes after fighting? Celebrating."

That got him frantic cheering.

"And what does every party worth the title need? Dancing!"

The cheers took on a deafening quality. Alerion realized Allienna had been right. The sound was addictive.

"Now, what many don't know is that I'm not only a skilled warrior but also quite the dancer." He winked in the direction of his mates, who were standing so close to the entrance they were almost inside the arena. They waved happily.

"I can see many of you are here as Vikings, so why don't we start with a traditional Viking dance? First, we need the rhythm." He motioned for four of the demons who were lined up around the arena to step forward. Another thing about demons, something nobody ever suspected, was that they were extremely musical. Why that was so remained a mystery, even to him. Perhaps to balance out the more destructive tendencies they showed as a species?

He demonstrated the rhythm he needed for this specific dance, and they took it up immediately, reproducing it by clapping their hands, scratching their scales with their claws and hammering their swords against some shields.

"Now for the steps…"

* * * *

"That was nice." Troy and Declan were snuggled right and left of Alerion when they stepped through time and space into their apartment. Troy yawned. "You do make a stunning figure as a dancer."

"Did you doubt it? Don't forget, I know every dance in existence." Alerion lifted a brow in mock anger.

He was exhausted and elated. The evening at the renaissance fair had been totally different from what he'd expected. He had arrived there ready to once again wrangle his unruly demons and had ended up teaching about three hundred humans, as well as the demons he had thought he would have to chastise, how to do Viking and Germanic dances. For the first time in what felt like forever, Alerion had had actual *fun* when dealing with his subjects. And said subjects had definitely been over the moon. He wondered if he should maybe try a different approach when dealing with them. It surely wouldn't always work. Conditions had been very favorable in this instance, but it was worth thinking about. Though before he could start evaluating his ruling style, he had to have a bath first—with his mates, because without them, it wouldn't be a proper bath, just getting wet in a fancy piece of porcelain.

"*Mrow.*"

Alerion stared at the source of the sound. The red tom was strolling toward them with an impatient expression.

"I think he's pissed we were gone so long." Declan looked down at the feline, who twitched his tail as if he wanted to confirm his assumption...or deny it...or he was just itchy...or that was what he always did at this time of night when the moon was waning. The tom was hard to read.

"Uhm, are you hungry?" Alerion looked down at the cat who was, technically, his, though he had the nagging suspicion that if any owning was indeed taking place, it was the other way around. The tom did this strange jittery thing where his tail, butt and hindlegs shivered as if he was being cold, but only in the back half of his body. "Food it is."

His mates followed him into the kitchen, while the tom ran between his legs, weaving in and out so quickly, Alerion was afraid he would fall over the furry obstacle. Once there, Declan got a can of cat food, Troy picked up the red bowl with the encrusted remains of the last meal, Alerion found a knife to get half of the can's contents out and the tom went on his hind legs, yowling loudly as if he were starving.

"The window was open the entire day. You could have easily caught one of those monster rats outside," Declan admonished the feline.

The tom flattened his one ear and hissed at Declan. Even though none of them was fluent in 'cat', the meaning was clear. Declan should go out and catch the rats if he thought it was that easy. Declan lifted his hands in surrender.

"Fine, I get it. No doubting the vicious tom in the house." He furrowed his brows. "We still haven't got a name for you." He turned to his mates. "We need a name for him."

Alerion started scraping out the cat food into the bowl. "Do you have any suggestions?"

"I don't know. Bastard? Beast? Killer? Death of Rats? Hey, that's actually a good one! Go, Sir Terry and all." Declan grinned.

Troy eyed the tom and shook his head. "I don't think he likes those."

Indeed, the tom's tail was swishing left to right, a sure sign he wasn't amused.

"Hmm, so nothing aggressive." Alerion parted the solid food in smaller bits. The tom liked it that way. "Your Majesty? That would definitely fit him. Or Emperor?"

The hissing was answer enough.

"Nuisance. That's perfect." Troy got a quick swipe from a paw for his troubles. "Fine. Sam? Brutus? Allie? Adam? Tenoch?"

None of the names Troy threw out found the tom's approval. Declan tried it with Bruce, Arthur, Tony, Bucky, and Peter, which the tom didn't even acknowledge. Alerion huffed. This cat was definitely high maintenance. Just to mess with him, Alerion suggested, "Well, if the names of literal heroes aren't acceptable, how about Mr. Fluffy Pants? Or Sparkles?"

"What makes you think of sparkles or fluff when looking at this cat?" Declan wanted to know. Before Alerion could answer, the tom yowled softly. He looked up at Alerion, clearly trying to communicate something.

"You like Fluffy Pants?" Alerion tried to confirm. The tom shook his head. He actually *shook* his head.

"Fluffy Sparkle?" Troy threw in. Again, a headshake.

"Mr. Fluffy Sparkle Pants?" Declan balled his fist in triumph when his suggestion was met with a satisfied purr. "Ha! I did it! I found his name!"

"Only because we eliminated the other possibilities. Lucky guess, I'd say." Troy was grumbling but not too loudly. Alerion had a feeling they were all glad to have found a name for the fourth member of their little family.

"Face it, I'm a genius." Declan did a little shimmy with his ass that had both Troy and Alerion forgetting all about names.

# Chapter Twelve

Declan sighed and burrowed deeper into Troy's side when the mattress dipped. He didn't know how late it was but definitely too early to get up. Troy mumbled something incoherent and snaked his arm around Declan's waist. Satisfied that at least one of his mates would be staying with him, Declan got ready to doze off.

He heard Alerion shuffling around the room, using the bathroom before he went to the kitchen where Mr. Fluffy Sparkle Pants made it known how terribly long it had been since his last meal. The starting of the coffee maker as well as the kettle announced the beginning of breakfast preparations. Perhaps they should help their mate with that...or not. After their lovemaking the previous night, Alerion probably wanted to show them how much he had appreciated their ministrations. It would be unfair to deprive him of this wonderful opportunity. And being in a relationship meant being considerate of all the tiny details so everybody was happy. Declan realized being a good mate wasn't as hard as he had thought it would be.

"We should help him." Troy's words yanked him from his fantasy land where his laziness was really love.

"I'm sure he wants to do this in appreciation of last night." Declan clung to Troy like a barnacle.

"Uhm, you mean he wants to thank us for some of the greatest orgasms *we* ever had because of his talented and very flexible tongue?"

"I sound like a horrible mate when you put it like that!"

"You're not horrible, just lazy as fuck. Now get your ass in gear. We need to help Alerion then we need to talk about his crisis management and what we're going to do about the council."

"That's too much! I can't handle so many things at once. It's too early!" Declan wasn't above whining. He'd never been a morning person, and his inner slouch was pretty sure that with two mates, he should get more lenience in the dreaded early hours.

"It's almost half past eight. Practically noon." Troy was merciless, always had been. Declan seriously wondered why he loved him so much. "Get your ass in gear. The quicker we get done, the sooner we can go back to bed and try our hand at tonguing."

Ah, yes, the man had brilliant ideas. That's why Declan loved him so much. He heaved himself off the bed, followed Troy into the bath where they did their thing before joining Alerion in the kitchen. Their mate was busy frying eggs and bacon in a pan while Mr. Fluffy Sparkle Pants was devouring his food.

After a delicious three-way kiss — the training was definitely paying off — Declan set the table while Troy manned the toaster.

Their coffee was ready when Alerion filled the plates with heaps of bacon and eggs. Troy placed the basket with the toast in the middle, and they all sat down to eat. Once the worst of his hunger was sated, Declan looked up from his plate of perfectly fried bacon. Alerion had this trick where it got extra crispy, and that alone was a reason to keep the man for good.

"Uhm, can we talk about your demons and our council? Or do you want to wait until we've eaten?"

Alerion swallowed the piece of buttered toast he'd had in his mouth. "I guess talking while we have something delicious to distract us a bit isn't a bad idea?"

"No, I guess not." Troy crunched a piece of bacon. "I love your bacon-making skills, by the way."

"Thank you, my love. I've had centuries to perfect them." Alerion winked. "Let's start with the council. I guess it's safe to say that by sending Tino and Jules, they've shown that they won't be leaving you alone anytime soon. You have been dealing with them for years. What's your contingency plan?"

"What makes you think we have one of those?" Declan grinned.

"We may have only been mated for two weeks, but that was long enough for me to know you have plans for several scenarios. And even if we weren't mated, what Sammy has told me about you two is enough for me to wish to never be on your bad side."

"Oooh, you say the nicest things." Troy leaned across the table to kiss Alerion. Declan followed his example before he started explaining their contingency plans to their stunningly clever mate.

"We have indeed more than one plan. So far, we were successful with simply ignoring them, but I guess those days are gone. The involvement of Tino and Jules makes us angry enough to seriously think about pulling the plug on them. Only problem is then we have lots of shifters running around without a ruling body. That's not our idea of fun, and we definitely don't want to step up. The goal is to get more free time to spend with you, not to accumulate more responsibilities."

"Hmm. That pulling of the plug, how would you do that?" Alerion was waving a piece of toast through the air. Movement in the corner of his eyes told Declan that Mr. Fluffy Sparkle Pants was very interested in where that morsel was going.

"We can ruin them financially within a week, tops. All we have to do is call Emilia, and we can start."

Alerion snickered. "I knew you wouldn't go the bloody route but hitting them where it definitely will hurt the most? You're geniuses. And for the record, I think involving Emilia is plain evil."

Troy and Declan both bowed. "Coming from you, that's high praise." Declan winked.

"I always give credit where credit is due. As for who is going to rule the shifter world... Why don't you find capable representatives who take care of things and report back to you? I'm sure there have to be some shifters around who know what they're doing."

Declan shared a look with Troy. "It's not a bad idea. I guess we just have to find them..."

Troy furrowed his brows. "Well, I guess making the effort of finding the right people will save us trouble and time in the future. But I want to talk to Tino and Jules first. Since they were sent by the council, they can surely give us some insights."

"Good idea." Alerion put the toast in his mouth, which made their feline family member growl.

They all stared at Mr. Fluffy Sparkle Pants, who was sitting on his haunches, clearly waiting to get food from the table. Alerion sighed. "If we start feeding you, you'll be insufferable in the future," he tried to explain to the tom.

Mr. Fluffy Sparkle Pants wasn't impressed. He hissed.

"I guess it's already too late for that. Welcome to our table." Alerion took the saucer from under his mug, filled it with bits of toast, egg and bacon and placed it in front of the demanding cat. A satisfied purr was the reward for his troubles.

"Now that we have something resembling a plan regarding the council, how are we going to get the demons under control?" Troy put the last bit of bacon into his mouth. "I guess finding responsible representatives is out of the question."

"Pretty much." Gloomily, Alerion stared into his tea. "Yesterday wasn't so bad. It showed they can adapt. I'm just afraid the risk is too high, because demons can be so excitable. And I still don't know how to tell Barion and Jon that *Demon Wars* needs to vanish from the market before the full version to the public has even launched."

Declan could feel the defeat radiating from their demonic mate. Alerion loved his sons and sons-in-law, and he was so proud of Barion's and Jon's accomplishments. Then it hit Declan like a brick in the face. He got so agitated, he thumped the table hard enough to send their mugs tumbling, spilling the remains of coffee and tea over the surface.

"Declan, what's the matter?" Troy put his mug back up. Luckily, there hadn't been enough liquid left in any of them to make a real mess. The spillage remained on the table.

"I'm a genius!"

"Uhm, we have discussed this before, Declan, babe. Jon is a genius because he can make computers do things we wouldn't even dream about. And Milo is a genius because he makes numbers dance to his tune. You're the best mate Alerion and I could wish for, and you're very intelligent, but a genius…?" Troy trailed off when Declan showed him the finger.

"I just found Alerion responsible representatives, which makes me a genius. So shut it."

"Huh? How did you do that? And more importantly, who?" Alerion was leaning forward, hope in his voice.

"Think about it. You've got three sons, two of which are happily mated to reasonably responsible people. Don't you think Dre and Barion can take over some of your duties? With the help of Sammy and Jon, of course. You could have like, a schedule of who's got to put out the fires when." Declan huffed in pride. His idea was brilliant, and he knew it!

Alerion tapped his lips with his right index finger. "Hmm. Not a bad idea. And I could involve them in the problem with *Demon Wars*. If they have to find a solution, perhaps we don't have to take it off the market. Or Barion and Jon realize themselves that this is the only solution, and I don't have to break their hearts…at least not directly. Not bad at all." He hesitated. "But let's leave Quirion out of it. For one, I can't imagine him leaving his precious library, and even if he does, I don't want to imagine what chaos *he* would rain when he's left unsupervised."

"Okay, so we have a plan for both our problems. Let's see if they can withstand reality. Also, I take back what I said. You are a genius!" Troy blew Declan a kiss. "Now let's tidy the kitchen and get down to Sammy's to talk to Tino and Jules."

\* \* \* \*

When they entered Sammy's bookstore, Troy immediately sensed Tino and Jules. The two omegas were sitting on the turquoise sofa, both wearing clothes they had clearly gotten from Sammy and drinking Sammy's delicious lattes. Sammy was behind the counter with Dre, preparing another mug for his mate, no doubt. The wind chime announcing their arrival made all four men turn their heads toward the door.

"Declan, Troy, Dad! I wish you a wonderful morning! Come in. Do you want coffee? We have strawberry muffins today. They're to die for. Well, not really, because when you're dead you can't eat them anymore, but they taste great." Sammy was beaming at them.

Dre simply nodded before returning to staring at his mate with a lovesick smile. Tino and Jules tensed, their stress a heavy perfume in the air. Troy held up his hands in a placating gesture.

"It's fine. A good morning to all of you, too. Yes, we never turn down a coffee from you, as you well know. Tino, Jules, don't worry. We'd like to talk to you and perhaps we can find a solution to this whole mess."

"Oh, about that... Tino, Jules and I talked. The very good news is they're not the least bit interested in you because you're A, taken and B, totally not their type. The very bad news is that the council has taken Tino's mom and Jules' little sister hostage to force them into breeding with you. It's so mean." Sammy was busy operating the coffee machine so he neither saw the shocked expressions on the two omegas' faces nor did he hear the angry snarls coming from Troy and his mates.

Of course, the council couldn't even find willing omegas to send to them. Though it was better this way, because Troy was pretty sure Tino and Jules would be happy to help them against the council.

"Sammy," Tino groaned, "we said we wanted to broach the topic carefully."

"But why?" Sammy turned around, the coffee sieve full of freshly ground beans in hand. "Troy and Declan and Dad need to know. I told you they have zero interest in turning you into breeding machines. Dad already has five sons," Troy could hear Alerion sighing happily next to him, because Sammy had included himself and Jon in his offspring. "And Declan and Troy have a lot of growing up to do before they should be thinking about babies. Plus, if they ever want to reproduce, they would want a willing surrogate, not somebody under duress." He turned back to making coffee.

Troy shook his head. "I'm a little offended about the growing up comment, but Sammy is right. We would never force anybody to have our children...if we ever want more."

Dre lifted a brow. The demon had immediately caught on to Troy's meaning. As had Alerion, who gasped happily. Their mate really was a family man through and through. Only Declan, the genius—*har, har*—needed things spelled out.

"Huh?"

"We're Alerion's mates. That makes us the stepdads of Dre, Barion and Quirion, as well as Jon and Sammy." Troy chuckled evilly when Declan's eyes widened in panic.

"I'm not going to send Dre into a time out!"

"And you don't have to, because our middle son is very well behaved. I credit Sammy for it." Alerion put his arms around Troy's and Declan's shoulders, then he turned toward Tino and Jules. "As you can see, we have all the family we need."

Jules huffed. "I'm so glad. There's no way we could have played the obedient omegas for any length of time. Yesterday was already hard."

"You mean yesterday was an act?" Troy wasn't as surprised as he probably should have been. Even when clouded by pheromones, his brain was good at picking up nuances in people's behavior, and Tino and Jules had been a bit odd, even when he factored in the stress they must have been under and despite their tears.

"Yep...totally." Tino shrugged. "If the council hadn't taken my mom and Jules' sister, we'd never have come here. We're both too busy. Jules is getting his degree in law, and I'm only four months away from finalizing my studies in business studies. We don't have time for alphas or babies."

"I can schee that, which brings us back to the most presching matter. Do you know where they're keeping your family membersch?" Declan's fangs were down because he was so furious. In his opinion, there was nothing worse than involving innocent people in something personal. Troy was of one mind with his mate in that regard.

"Yes. They have them in the office building in New York. Officially, they're guests, but they can't leave their rooms and aren't allowed to talk to anybody." Jules was snarling, showing more aggressive behavior than Troy would have thought possible for an omega. Then again, what he knew about omegas was restricted to what his parents and the elders had told him — a lot of obviously outdated BS, which most probably had never held much truth to begin with.

He felt slightly ashamed that he and Declan had never looked more deeply into the lives of omegas. His wolf definitely thought their well-being was part of his duties, though he'd never been vocal about it until now. It was a bad case of out of sight, out of mind. By leaving shifter society behind, they had also turned their back on those who didn't have the power to simply walk out. It was a mistake on their part, one they would correct now.

"Do you know how heavily they are guarded?" Alerion sounded very calm. Troy was sure their battle-hardened mate was already coming up with several rescue plans.

"Who's heavily guarded?" The chimes gave a nice musical background to the question. They all turned to see Emilia, Mavis and Maribel entering the shop. Emilia lifted a perfectly curved brow. "And who are your charming guests?" She smiled at Tino and Jules, who got up from the couch to greet the newcomers.

"And why do we sense war in the air?" Mavis was already on her way to the counter, patting Alerion on his back in passing before she took one of the strawberry muffins. After a tentative sniff, she bit into it.

"The rumors are true. These are better than our recipe. This cannot be!" She turned to her lover and fellow witch, Maribel, who had greeted the omegas, slapped Declan's ass with a wink and given Sammy a kiss across the counter, ignoring Dre's barely restrained growl. Apparently, the witches were on fire today.

"Then take two of those muffins with you so we can analyze the ingredients and do one better. Also, who are we going up against?" Maribel smiled broadly at everybody present.

From the moment they had joined the book club, Troy had known they could rely on all its members to have their backs. The readiness with which the witches and Emilia were willing to go against an unknown enemy with them warmed his heart.

"Uhm, we better start at the beginning." Troy gestured at the sofas. "Why don't we all sit down?"

"I'm making everybody's favorite drink!" Sammy announced, which sealed the deal. Once they were all seated, properly introduced and the drinks served — Alerion moaned into his chili chocolate almost as passionately as he had done the night before in the tub — Troy looked at his two mates, who nodded for him to do the explaining.

"Okay, so Declan and I had hoped the Shifter Council wouldn't find out about our mating with Alerion for the next thousand years, which was wishful thinking on our part. Apparently when the uber alphas mate, every shifter gets a magical notification." He was still pissed about that. It was as if Fenris had never heard about privacy laws — which he probably hadn't. Still...

Maribel *tsk*ed. "We could have told you that, if you had asked." She grinned saucily. "Which you couldn't, because you were otherwise occupied."

Emilia groaned. "Stop putting images in my head, I'm begging you!"

"Please, darling, three hot men of the paranormal persuasion in one bed? What's not to like?" Mavis blew on her tea.

"Because we're going to meet in three days to discuss *Alice's Adventures in Wonderland*, and I want to be able to focus on the topic and not have a hardcore porno running amok in my head!" Emilia twirled one lock of her gorgeous hair around her slender forefinger.

"What kind of hardcore porno?" Mavis asked, clearly interested.

"Please, can we stay on topic? And for the record, I'm with Emilia on this one. I do *not* want an imagine of my dads having sex in my head!" Dre clung to Sammy as if he could save him from the mental torture.

"I just want to point out that any porno starring us would be Oscar-worthy," Alerion chimed in.

"Yes, totally. Now please let's get back to waging war against whoever pissed you off. I assume it was the shifter council?" Emilia glanced at Tino and Jules, who had been watching the entire conversation with wide-eyed fascination. It could be overwhelming in the beginning, Troy had to admit. And Amber, Barion and Jon weren't even there.

"Okay, where were we? Ah, yes, the shifters knew instantly, and an elder called Simarl called us to invite us to some official shindig to celebrate our mating to an omega."

"But Alerion isn't— Oh. *Oh!*" Emilia started grinning, her long fangs fully out.

"I'm so glad our predicament is so much fun for you," Declan snapped with no real heat. Until the council had decided to involve Tino and Jules, they had seen it more as a pesky fly they could swat away any time they wished. With the lives and well-being of innocents on the line, the matter had become a lot more serious.

"Let me guess... They didn't take Alerion being an alpha very well?" Maribel shook her head. "Of course they didn't. Shifters have always been a bit... traditional."

"Just like vampires, really," Emilia grumbled. "Seems to be the one thing both species have in common."

"Oh, don't feel bad, darling. Witches can be freaking stubborn as well." Mavis sighed. "I guess longevity isn't a guarantee for tolerance. The tendency to cling to the familiar is too tempting. Back to the council." She nodded at Troy to continue.

"Anyway, when they realized we wouldn't start producing babies in ever, they lost it. We told them, or rather Elder Simarl, off and thought we might have a few decades until they came up with the next stupid idea. We were wrong."

All eyes went to Tino and Jules, who both held up their hands.

"Hey," Tino started. "We already told you that we wouldn't even be here if they hadn't taken our mom and sister."

"They took hostages?" Emilia's smooth voice now carried the undertones of death and destruction. A pissed-off vampire was never a pretty sight. A pissed-off vampire from the oldest bloodline? Even Troy's wolf was a bit wary.

"Yes. My mom and Jules' sister." Tino looked equally angry and devastated.

It broke Troy's heart.

"We're going to get them back." Sammy, who was sitting next to the omegas, put his hand on Tino's leg in a comforting gesture.

"Uh, you won't be doing anything dangerous, *mo grah thu*," Dre stressed, stroking Sammy's nape. "But we will bring the hostages back." To emphasize his words, his fangs dropped, and his scales came out in full glory.

"That's my son!" Alerion beamed. "And Dre is right, Sammy, my dearest. You stay here with Tino and Jules while we free their family members."

"Oh no! We want to help!" Tino and Jules both protested loudly. Their muscles were rippling, a clear sign of how close to shifting they were.

Troy looked first at Declan then at Alerion. Things were getting slightly out of hand. "First, we need a solid plan. Then we can decide who gets to come and who stays here."

"Do we have a plan?" Mavis had taken her knitting work out of her ginormous handbag. Knowing how much damage the woman could do with a finely woven spell, Troy tried to rein her in. A deep voice from the back of the shop cut him off.

"What plan?" Barion and Jon stepped into the lounging area. Sammy jumped up to greet Jon with a hug before he went behind the counter to make drinks for the newcomers.

*Wonderful, now we're only missing Amber*, Troy thought.

"Why did I have the urgent feeling to come here?" the banshee's voice droned over the wind chime. The gang was complete.

"Hi, Amber, it's nice to see you. Jon, Barion." Troy nodded at them all.

"There's trouble, isn't there?" Amber plonked herself down next to Emilia, nudging the vampire in a way that was too intimate to be insignificant. Troy might not be a genius, but he was wise enough to not comment. Instead, he quickly filled the newcomers in on what they had discussed so far, managing to do so with being interrupted only twice. That had to be a new record.

"What's the plan?" Amber was sipping her chai latte, her free hand playing with the hem of Emilia's plaid shirt.

"We haven't formulated one yet. There are several options." Alerion stared longingly into his empty cup. "Sammy, could you?" He held it out to his son-in-law, who jumped up with a smile.

"Of course, Dad. The same again?"

"Yes, please."

Sammy got busy behind the counter, closely watched by his mate.

"Options?" Mavis probed.

"Ah, yes. Well, the first one is something Declan and I have been preparing for since we cut ties with the council." Troy nodded at Emilia. "With Emilia's help, we were able to get the majorities in every business the council elders are involved in. We can completely ruin them financially within a week."

Emilia's grin was positively savage. "Which would be almost as much fun as eviscerating them all."

"Emilia! Blood should be a last resort." Sammy looked at her from his coffee machine, and the vampire actually looked contrite.

"Sorry, Sammy. You're right, of course."

"If you feel violent, perhaps you want to try this chocolate chip cookie? It's made with extra chocolate for more flavor." Sammy got out a plate and put two large discs of softly baked dough on it. Dre got up to retrieve it and the scents wafting in their direction made Troy's wolf perk up. Sammy, who always seemed to know what others needed, prepared several more plates with different pastries, which Dre served. The violent undercurrents in the room eased significantly. Such was the power of sugar and fat.

"Okay, bathing in the blood of your enemies is out," Maribel remarked with a wink. "Hitting them with the loss of money sounds like a great idea, though I wouldn't advise doing that while they still have hostages."

"True. How shall we proceed?" Barion looked around.

"First, we need to know the layout of the main office in New York where they are being held." Declan tapped his chin with his finger. "Tino, Jules, can you help us there?"

The two omegas shrugged. "We've only been there once, when they showed us the rooms in which they were keeping my mom and his sister." Tino looked angry just talking about it. "We can describe the entrance area and the elevator we took upstairs. That's all, I'm afraid."

"Damn. Okay, Jon, can you hack the security cams in the building?"

Jon nodded. "Sure. Let me get my laptop."

"Already on it." Barion sliced space and time, popped out and in within a minute. "Here you go, *iubit*."

"Thank you, B." Jon took the laptop, opened it and started dancing his fingers over the keyboard. "Address?" He looked at Tino and Jules.

They rattled off where the main office of the shifter council was located and a few minutes later Jon huffed in triumph. He typed a bit more before he turned the laptop for everybody to see. "Here we go."

They all studied the different camera feeds, including one with the two unwilling guests. Tino's mother seemed very composed, or perhaps she had despaired because she was just sitting at the small table in the sparse room, staring at the wall. Tino sobbed. "Mom."

"Do you think they drugged her with something?" Alerion was in full demon form, the shreds of his T-shirt hung limply from his torso while the sweatpants he'd been wearing were stretched to the very limit.

"No. Wolves generally don't do well when locked up, but my mom gets claustrophobic then kind of shuts down." Tears were streaming down Tino's cheeks.

"We'll get her as soon as possible." Declan put a hand on the distraught omega's shoulder.

In the next feed, they saw Jules' sister. She was pacing her room, snarling at the camera now and then, looking all kinds of pissed off, which Troy could relate to very much.

"How old is she?" The question came from Sammy, and he sounded so unhappy that Troy wanted to soothe him immediately.

"She's twelve...and an omega." Jules chuckled helplessly. "Not that it stops her from being all fierce, obviously."

Declan put a hand on Jules' shoulder as well. "Don't worry. We'll get them out."

# Chapter Thirteen

Alerion saw the suffering of the two omegas and that of his mates, and he was furious. The urge to deal with the council in a permanent way was great. The only thing holding him back was the grief he would cause Sammy in doing so.

"If you give us an hour, we can compose some nice curse spells." Maribel was knitting so fast that her needles blurred a little.

"That's very nice of you, but you can take your time." Alerion cracked his knuckles. "Dre and I are getting the mom and the sister now. What are their names, by the way?"

"My mom's name is Phyllis."

"My sister is Lilly."

"Excellent. Dre? Are you ready? Mavis, Maribel, I think we might still need those curses. I don't know about you, but kidnapping members of their own species to blackmail other members of their own species isn't something that can be repented by simply losing all their money. There needs to be an extra edge…" Alerion let the sentence hang in the air.

Both witches chuckled. "We'll let our creativity flow. Now, go get them!"

Alerion felt two sets of hands on his back. "Be careful, mate." Declan pressed a kiss on his nape.

"Yeah, make it quick." Troy kissed Alerion's shoulder.

"Why does he get to come with you and not me?" Barion stood there pouting.

"Because there are only two hostages, which means two demons are needed." Alerion knew his youngest son. A tantrum was brewing.

"I could go with Dre." Yes, petulance was seeping into Barion's voice.

"No, Barion, son. Just think about it. You're a werewolf who's been imprisoned for a few days. You're nervous, frightened. Then a demon pops into your room out of nowhere to snatch you away. I think that's traumatic enough. We don't need *two* demons making it all worse."

Barion huffed. "Fine, I can see your point." He cocked his head. An adventurous gleam entered his eyes — a gleam Alerion had learned to fear. It meant his youngest son would blurt out a suggestion that sounded all logical and mature at first glance but was, at its core, the height of stupidity.

"No. I don't want to hear it. Dre and I are going now, and we'll be back before you're even done formulating whatever harebrained idea you just had." Alerion softened the blow of his words with a quick kiss to Barion's forehead.

"But it's a damn good idea! I thought all three of us could go, and we can take Tino and Jules with us, so Phyllis and Lilly won't be afraid."

Alerion had to give it to Barion. He obviously had thought this one through. Tino and Jules were giving him pleading looks, and Sammy was clapping his hands. "It's a wonderful idea. Nobody needs to get a trauma from being rescued by stunningly handsome demons."

Dre kissed Sammy on the top of his head, chuckling softly. "I hate to tell you this, *mo grah thu*, but apart from you and Jon — and now Declan and Troy — most people view demons as fearsome, not handsome."

"I don't understand it." Sammy snuggled against Dre's chest. "What's not to love? Gorgeous scales, hard muscles, inbuilt heating blanket and the brains to round out the entire package."

"Mmm, I love how you love all aspects of my demonic nature." Dre started nuzzling Sammy's neck and Alerion knew he had to intervene quickly or things would get out of hand.

"Dre, we have hostages to rescue."

"Uh, sorry. I got carried away." Dre dropped his hands from Sammy's hips, squared his shoulders and nodded at Tino and Jules. "Let's do this." He let one of his claws come out. "I'll take Phyllis, if that's okay with you, Dad."

Alerion nodded. Dre might be easily distracted by Sammy's allure, but he could focus if he put his heart in it. "Tino, you go with Barion and Dre. Jules, you're with me. I'm going to open a rift in space and time, and I want you to step through it before me. That way, the first thing your sister sees is you, not a monster she might want to attack."

Both omegas nodded, looking determined. Going in with three demons was still overkill, even if having backup was a nice touch.

Alerion sliced time and space the same moment Dre did. Tino and Jules stepped through, closely followed by their demonic guards. When he entered the room where Lilly was held, she was already in the arms of her brother, admonishing him.

"I hope you didn't do what this bunch of assholes has demanded. You need to finish your studies, not get pregnant by some overbearing alphas!"

Alerion already liked Lilly a lot.

"I did what they asked, because they had you, Lilly. Luckily for both of us, the uber alphas are happily mated and have no interest in siring pups, which is the reason I'm here. Their mate, Alerion, and his sons are breaking you and Phyllis out."

Alerion cleared his throat to announce his presence. Lilly looked up from where she was hugging her brother.

Her eyes rounded.

Alerion braced himself for fearful screaming, reminding himself that it was an unfortunate yet not ungrounded prejudice against his kind at work and not something personal. The squeal coming from Lilly hit tones he was barely able to hear, then she abandoned her brother to grab Alerion's hand and shake it.

"Oh, this is soooo exciting. I've always wanted to meet a demon. There are so many stories about you guys. Tell me, is it true you can go into other dimensions? Can you take me? I want to see it all. Everything that's out there! Jules, this is the best day of my life!"

Alerion looked at Jules over Lilly's head, and he shrugged. "Sorry," he mouthed.

Alerion winked. There was nothing to be sorry for. It was nice not being feared for a change. He looked up to where the camera was mounted.

"I guess we'd better get going. They probably have somebody watching the feeds." As if to confirm his suspicions, they heard trampling and shouting outside.

Lilly started to growl, and her small hands that had been holding on to Alerion's started to get furry. With a quick sweep, Alerion opened a new passage back to Beaconville and Sammy's bookshop.

They were greeted with cheers and shouts. Dre, Barion, Tino and Phyllis were already there, standing close to the counter where Sammy was busy making another beverage, this time obviously for Phyllis, who already looked a lot better than on the videos of only a few minutes ago. Alerion was tackled by his mates, who grabbed him from both sides, raining kisses on his cheeks. He smiled. Was there a better way to celebrate the successful conclusion of a mission? Even if said mission had been a simple in and out.

"You were great, babe." Troy beamed at him.

"Yes, a total badass." Declan rubbed his lower back.

"Thank you." It was Phyllis who had left the counter with a huge mug of steaming black tea in her hand, if Alerion's nose was to be trusted, to stand in front of him. Now it was Lilly who got to choose her drink.

"It was my pleasure." Alerion bowed. "And my sons'."

Phyllis looked at Declan and Troy. "Tino says you do not wish to breed him." The words sounded strangely old-fashioned and formal, leaving a bad aftertaste in Alerion's mouth from all the implications riding on them.

Declan shook his head. "No, we do not wish to sire any pups at this moment. And if we ever decide to have offspring, you can be certain we won't force anybody to carry them."

Phyllis sighed. "You're not as the council described you."

"Is that so? What does the council have to say about us?" Troy's voice had a growly undertone.

Phyllis winced and Troy immediately apologized. "I'm sorry. I'm not angry at you."

"I understand." Phyllis sipped her tea. A smile blossomed on her face. "This is good!"

"Thank you!" Sammy had left the counter to stand next to Dre and Barion. Lilly had sat next to Emilia and Amber, staring at them with wide, gleaming eyes. It seemed demons weren't the only creatures she'd always wanted to meet.

"Back to the council." Declan's muscles were tense where Alerion was stroking him gently on his upper arm.

"They say you're getting ready to lead all shifters into a war against the humans and the other paranormal species — that you're going to conquer the entire world and sire pups until the next uber alpha is born."

"That's what *they* want." Troy's fists were balled. "We just want to be left in peace, to enjoy life with our mate and our friends."

Phyllis visibly relaxed. "I was worried — and I wasn't the only one. Most shifters don't want a war."

"Then we have good news. There won't be one." Troy patted her shoulder. "Now let's sit down, and you tell us everything the council has done to you. Then we decide how to best punish them." He gestured toward the sofas.

Looking at them, Alerion realized things would be *very* cozy. Even though the three couches were big, there were just too many people present. Sammy solved this problem by dragging out two beanbags before he plopped down on Dre's lap. Lilly grabbed one of the bags and got comfortable at the feet of Emilia and Amber, who smiled at the young werewolf indulgently. Jules took the other one to sit next to his sister. Jon used Barion as his seat, which freed up enough room for everybody else to find a spot.

"Now, Phyllis, Lilly, we know the past few days must have been hard for you, and if you're not ready to talk about certain things, we fully understand. It would help us a great deal, though, if you could share any information or insights you have." Declan was so empathic, and Alerion felt his heart swell in pride. He had really won the jackpot in the mate department.

"Oh, believe me, I'll gladly live through all this again if it helps getting rid of those fucking morons." Lilly bared her teeth, and her fangs were slightly elongated. "They grabbed me on my way home from school. You know, our parents don't have a lot of money. They both work two jobs to get Jules and me through school and college, and that's why I have to take the bus, because both Mom and Dad are at work most of the time." She looked at Jules, who grabbed her hand and squeezed. "I had just gotten off the bus at my station when three alphas jumped out of the bushes and explained to me that I had to go with them. The assholes thought I'd come quietly, ha."

"What did you do?" Troy leaned forward in his seat.

"I asked them how high they thought the chances were that nobody would come if I started to scream. We don't live in the best neighborhood, but it's not yet a ghetto. They got pissy and told me it was orders from the council. I asked them to show me their IDs and to tell me why exactly the council wanted to see me, of all people." Lilly took a huge gulp of her hot chocolate. "Of course they didn't have IDs, because they were operating 'under the radar', as they called it. I was seriously thinking about running away, because no way would they have been able to catch me in my hood, but they started threatening Mom and Dad, so I went with them."

"You were very brave." Declan smiled at her.

"Yeah, if I'd known they would blackmail Jules, I'd have scratched their eyes out."

For a twelve-year-old, Lilly was pretty aggressive and mature, Alerion realized. It was no doubt because as an omega, she had to fight for everything thrice as hard as everybody else.

"What about you, Phyllis?" Troy looked at Tino's mother. Before she could answer, his cell started blasting what Alerion assumed was a song, though only because he didn't think his mate had recorded an actual tanker being slowly crushed by a metal press.

"Oooh, cool, that's *Decency Defied* by Cannibal Corpse, isn't it?" Tino clapped his hands. "I love that band."

"Finally, somebody with great taste in music!" Troy winked. "Yes, that's Cannibal Corpse. I thought this ringtone was perfect for the council." He got his cell out. "Shall we see what they want?" The gleam in his eyes said he could make a good guess concerning the reason for this call, as they all could. Emilia grinned with her fangs fully out.

"Pleasche, put it on schpeaker."

"As you wish." Troy pressed the green icon as well as the one that put the call on speaker. Then he placed the cell on the table with Drogon and Smaug.

"Elder Simarl, to what do we owe this call?" he greeted the caller. Alerion assumed it was always the same person from the council calling his mates for Troy to know the name.

"Alphas, something terrible has happened!" The elder sounded so righteously indignant that Alerion had to suppress a snicker. One look around their group confirmed he wasn't the only one.

The elder droned on. "No less than an hour ago, three demons invaded our main office in New York and kidnapped two shifters in our care."

"Oh no! That sounds serious, Elder Simarl. You don't happen to know who these demons were?" Troy was a gifted actor, Alerion realized, full of awe. His tone had almost fooled him, and it obviously did the elder.

"I'm afraid you wouldn't believe me, Alpha." The elder was good at building up to the main point. Alerion had to give him that.

"We can't believe anything if we don't hear it." Declan, on the other hand, was good at crushing the elder's momentum.

The annoyed huff coming from the other end of the line made clear how little the elder appreciated Declan's gift. "It was your so-called mate and two of his sons. This was clearly an act of aggression. If you ask me, the demon king was just waiting for his chance to start a take-over of the shifter world."

Alerion lifted a brow. He had wondered how the council would play this. Trying to start a war right off the bat was ambitious, to put it mildly. Alerion decided to find out what kinds of drugs shifters could smoke to get this delusional at the earliest chance he got.

"These are serious allegations, Elder Simarl. Not only against our mate and his sons — who, I might add, are our sons through the mating bond — but also against his entire species. This could lead to war." Troy was clearly aiming for an Oscar. He sounded so genuinely worried, as if he actually believed what the elder was saying.

"I know." Simarl couldn't quite leave the smugness out of his voice. *No Oscar for him, then.* Also, how did he think shifters would fare against demons should they really decide to become hostile? The stupidity and willful carelessness of this so-called leader stunned Alerion into speechlessness.

"I'm sure you have proof to back up your claims, Elder?" Troy had shifted into business mode, no doubt to get things moving. It was already past noon, and despite the pastries Sammy had so generously given out, they all could do with lunch. Plus, Sammy had closed his shop for the time being, missing out on business because of the council. Alerion made a mental note to make sure to reimburse his son for the troubles they had brought to his doorstep.

He understood that Sammy made most of his money online, brokering antique books and rare mangas, which always seemed to find a way into his loving embrace before he found them the perfect new owners, but he also loved having customers in his store. And there were several people, especially teenagers, for whom the store was a sanctuary. They usually started coming after school, which left them a couple of hours, but still… Listening to this elder was tiring.

"Yes, of course I have proof. The rooms the two wolves were taken from were under video surveillance. We have it all on tape."

"Excellent. Though I do need to ask why you would have cameras in ordinary rooms?" Declan lifted a brow, more for the audience around the two tables than for the elder, who couldn't see him anyway.

"That's…uhm. That is…you see… We have all rooms under surveillance. It's standard procedure."

Which was a blatant lie, evidenced by the stammering and the waver in the elder's voice. Shifters were notoriously bad at lying. It was an art they never bothered to learn, because why go to the trouble when the people around you could smell it on you?

"Ah, protocols must have changed since we last had the pleasure of visiting one of the offices." Declan winked at Troy, who showed his teeth. Both his mates weren't too happy with the council.

"Yes, yes. After all, tight security is invaluable." Simarl was back on solid ground — or so he thought.

"Then why don't you send us the video feeds right now so we can verify your allegations and talk to our mate? If even only a part of what you said is true, we need to act fast." Troy was talking business again, calmly cornering the elder. There was no way he could send the surveillance right now. Even a gifted hacker would need some time to tamper with it and cut out Tino and Jules. Barion's idea to take the two omegas with them had been brilliant in more ways than one. Perhaps he owed his son an apology.

"You see, we can't send it right away. The files are…huge and —"

"Don't worry, Elder. Declan's and my computers are both high end and able to process vast amounts of data. Just send it and let us take care of the rest."

"This is not—"

"Oh, why, Elder, don't tell me you don't actually have any proof? You wouldn't have lied to your alphas, would you?" Troy obviously had fun twisting the knife, much to the amusement of their audience. They were all trying valiantly to suppress their snickers.

"We have proof!" Simarl was quick to shout. "It's just not... Just not..."

"Just not adequately edited for us to see," Declan suggested in a cheerful tone. "I guess you haven't erased Tino and Jules from the footage yet? Or how a bunch of heavily armed guards entered both rooms shortly after Phyllis and Lilly were rescued? By the way, they are fine. We've already talked to them at length, and I can't say it's looking good for you, Elder— or anybody else on the council. Kidnapping and blackmail? Forced pregnancies? *Tsk, tsk.* Not what we would expect from people who, as you have often claimed for yourself, are our humble representatives."

"This makes us seriously doubt if you're fit to lead in our stead. You will, of course, get a chance to defend your actions. Let's say in four days? We're going to come to the main office at three a.m. sharp, so be ready explain to us why exactly you thought it necessary to kidnap a busy mother and a minor and why you sent two omegas drenched in pheromones to us. I can't say King Alerion was overly happy about this blatant attempt at interfering with our mating." Not giving the elder another chance to say something, Troy ended the call.

For a moment, there was silence. Then Amber started giggling, quickly followed by Emilia, the witches then all the others. It was good, laughing with friends, cleansing. Alerion felt the rage about the elders' meddling subside in the presence of his friends and family.

Declan was the first to sober up. "Now, I don't think it's a good idea for Phyllis and Lilly to go back home yet. Neither for you two." He eyed Jules and Tino.

"They can stay here." Sammy got up from his perch on Dre's knees, smiling at the four werewolves. "I have a guestroom where two of you can stay, and Jon and Barion have another one."

Phyllis glanced at her son, who shared a quick look with Jules. "We're very grateful, Sammy, Jon. I think Mom and I would take Sammy's room, if that's okay. I don't want her in the cellar. She's been caged enough as it is."

Phyllis shuddered a bit at his words.

"No problem." Jules smiled reassuringly. "Lilly and I can go downstairs." He nodded at Barion and Jon. "Thanks for having us."

"Don't mention it. We're glad we can help." Barion smiled down on Jon, who was snuggled against his chest.

"Wonderful." Alerion rubbed his hands. "Now that all this is cleared up, my mates and I can go back home and enjoy our mating."

"Uhm, gladly, Alerion, honey, but we still need to read *Alice's Adventures in Wonderland* for the day after tomorrow." Troy gave him a quick peck on the cheek.

"Oh." Alerion felt disappointment heavy in his chest. It was Sammy who brought back the sunshine.

"Why don't you come to the book club as well, Dad? I know you always have a lot to do, but now that Declan and Troy are your mates, perhaps you can slow down a bit?"

"Would you mind?" Alerion searched the faces of the book club members and those of his mates.

"No, definitely not. The more the merrier." Mavis beamed.

The others gave their enthusiastic consent as well, making Alerion the newest member of the group.

After a round of farewells to everybody, they returned back to their apartment, where Mr. Fluffy Sparkle Pants was already waiting, making clear what he thought of them leaving him alone and without food for more than half a day, which, in cat time, seemingly translated into an eternity.

# Chapter Fourteen

"Come on. Hurry, Troy." Declan watched as Alerion was hopping from one foot to the other, his copy of *Alice's Adventures in Wonderland* clutched tight to his massive chest. Their mate was anxious to get to his first book club meeting, which Declan found adorable. Who would have thought the mighty and feared demon king couldn't wait to discuss the finer points of a children's novel from 1865? The past two days had been rather quiet on the demon front, giving them time to read the book between hot make-out sessions and even hotter sex. If it hadn't been for the upcoming confrontation with the council, Declan would have said that those had been the most perfect days in his life so far. Spending them with both his mates in utter bliss was how he had always imagined his future life to be.

The three of them had already decided on a course of action, which made Declan's wolf anxious to implement their plan. The waiting made neither Declan nor his wolf or Troy and Alerion happy, but they had more or less promised the council four days — and those four days they would get.

It also gave Declan, Troy and Emilia the time to prepare the financial ruin of the council members and Mavis and Maribel a chance to be creative with their spell work. If only the waiting wasn't so tedious.

"I'm done. I'm done." Troy stepped out of the bathroom in tight jeans that had Declan instantly thinking of much better things than the council and the boredom of waiting. Judging from the growl coming from Alerion, their gorgeous demon mate had ideas as well.

"I thought we needed to get going?" Troy winked at them both.

"You terrible, terrible tease!" Declan groaned. "How are we supposed to think about a girl chasing after a white rabbit and falling down a seemingly endless hole if we have *this* to stare at?"

Troy shrugged. "You have this to look forward to. How about that?" He spun around, presenting them with his very tight ass in the painted-on denim.

"I guess this is going to be a short meeting." Alerion grabbed Troy around the waist, pulled him close and kissed him hard before spinning him around to Declan to do the same. Once Troy was sufficiently kissed, ramping up all three of them, they tried to get their raging hormones back under control before Alerion opened a rift. Declan really loved his friends from the book club, but he knew all too well how merciless the teasing would be if they arrived there with visible boners and reeking of unfulfilled sex.

"Perhaps we should take a cold shower before we go?" he suggested.

Alerion looked at the clock. "No time, beloved. *Someone* took far too long in the bathroom."

"You make it sound as if I was doing it on purpose." Troy huffed, playing the offended party so very well, even though all three of them had become remarkably good at initiating games in the bedroom — or under the shower, or in the living room, or one remarkable time in the hallway.

Always provided their red-furred pet was well fed and would therefore not act as an effective cockblocker.

"Think of our last board meeting with that company in France or imagine what your demons might come up with next, then how you're going to send Barion or Dre to deal with it." Troy winked at them both.

Declan grunted because just thinking about those entitled bastards in France had his erection sagging more quickly than a balloon after a hot needle had been stuck in. And Alerion wasn't faring any better. They had yet to talk to Dre and Barion about them helping their father, and imagining what mischief the demon subjects would come up with next was migraine inducing.

"Thank you. I'm good to go now." Alerion looked a bit sadly down to his crotch. "It was a good erection. Very promising."

"We can revive it later. Pinkie swear." Troy wove his arm through Alerion's. Declan hurried to follow his example and the next moment they stood in front of the coffee table in Sammy's book shop. Their mugs with coffee and hot chocolate were ready, indicating where they would be sitting. They greeted Mavis and Maribel, who were snuggled up on the turquoise sofa, leaving enough room for Emilia and Amber, who had just entered the shop. Once the greetings were out of the way and everybody was seated, Sammy opened the discussion.

"I'm so happy we're discussing *Alice's Adventures in Wonderland* today. Even though it was written a hundred and seventy-five years ago, it's still entertaining and fascinating — a real classic in English literature."

"I like that there's so many movie adaptations of the story and that it was even used as a reference in *Resident Evil*. I absolutely adore the Cheshire Cat in the movie from 2010 — close to the original but with a dark, modern twist." Barion took a huge bite of his mini cherry pie, devouring more than half of it in one go.

"Well, one of the hallmarks of truly timeless topics and stories is the fact that they are transferable into new times. Just take Dracula or Captain Ahab from *Moby Dick*, who are still recognized in our world. And who hasn't dreamed of falling before?" Amber tapped her fingers on the cover of her worn paperback edition. "I love how Lewis Carroll managed to combine the absurdity of the dream world with real life references and even smuggle nightmares in."

"I assume you're referring to the Tea Party, among others and the Queen of Hearts." Troy nodded, all serious. "Also, my personal favorite is the White Rabbit. I dig the vest."

"I love how many of the characters are modelled after real life people Alice Liddell, the girl for who Lewis Carroll wrote the story, knew in some capacity. I think I read somewhere that he himself was portrayed as the Dodo, because he stuttered." Jon was soft-spoken, as always.

Since he had mated with Barion, he was coming out of his shell more often, though when it came to the book club, he was still shy about sharing his thoughts. No doubt to reward him for his participation, Barion gave his mate a loud kiss on his cheek.

"My favorite character is the Caterpillar. A smoking arthropod on a mushroom? What a genius idea." Emilia sighed dreamily.

"Makes you wonder what Carroll smoked when he came up with the different characters." Mavis snickered. "Though probably nothing as good as these cream cheese pies. Barion, well done!"

It had been Barion's turn to get the snacks for the evening. Apparently, the demon had taken Dre's threats to heart and not tried to bake something himself. A quick tour through France and Belgium had provided them with various delicious pastries, which made it hard for Declan to decide what to try next.

The blue demon bowed elegantly in Mavis' direction. "I aim to please."

"Oh, you're *very* pleasing," Amber assured him. Dre huffed.

"Do I need to remind you of the selection of pancakes and truffles I brought to the last meeting? You said *I* was the best."

"And you are, my mate—for me, anyway." Sammy snuggled into Dre's side.

"Yes, Dre, that should be more than enough. Leave some glory for the rest of us." Barion stuck his tongue out, which Dre reacted to by flipping him the bird.

"I can't believe we managed almost fifteen minutes of earnest discussion," Troy muttered.

Declan felt a grin tugging at his lips. This was what he loved most about their meetings—the easy bantering between creatures of equal power. Nobody else would dare talk to him or Troy like the other members of the book club did. It was absolutely refreshing.

"Well, you can kiss that glory goodbye, because next time I'm going to bring the snacks and make you two look like the children you are." Alerion grabbed another cream cheese pie from the table and held it up. "These are delicious, no doubt, though nothing compared to what I'm going to bring!"

"Zenobia won't bake for you. We already tried," Dre announced with a smug grin.

Declan remembered Sammy telling him about Zenobia, high priestess of the goddess, who had a small restaurant in Rome. She was rumored to be one of the best cooks on Earth—or so Sammy had claimed. Apparently, Dre knew what his father had been planning. Alerion though, mature adult that he was, didn't seem fazed by his son's obvious glee.

"First of all, what makes you think I'd go to Zenobia? And second, she and I go way further back than you and her. I'm not above pulling favors."

"She said to me and Barion, and I quote, '*Do not for one second think I will use my gifts to make you two look good in front of your mates. You have to accomplish that on your own.*'" Dre crossed his arms in front of his chest.

"Ah, that's Zenobia as we know and love her." Maribel giggled. "She wants the demons to grow up!"

"As my sons should." Alerion sat very straight in his seat on the sofa, causing Declan and Troy to hang on to him. "It's an entirely different story when the king of all demons comes calling."

"Are you sure? Last time I checked, Zenobia was harder to sway than a marble statue." Barion gave Dre a high five, their previous squabble already forgotten.

"We shall see." Alerion still sounded absolutely sure, looking every inch the king that he was. Declan felt his blood heading south.

Emilia wrinkled her nose. "Can we get back to the topic at hand? Before our werewolves start an orgy."

"I'm wounded, Emilia." Troy clutched imaginary pearls. He did have a real set Declan had bought him for his birthday two years before, but he only ever wore them in the bedroom as his only clothing, an image that didn't help Declan's arousal. "We're still in the honeymoon phase. Let us have some fun."

"You can have as much fun as you want but not during the book club." Emilia was decisive.

"Oh, I don't know. A little man-on-man action has never hurt anybody." Mavis was pulling Maribel close.

"And I'm out." Barion got up, dragging Jon with him. "I'm really happy you found your mates, Dad, but I draw the line at witnessing said happiness in the flesh, so to speak. There are things no child should ever know about their father. Am I right, Dre?"

"This once I completely agree with you, Barion. Parents don't have sex." The huge red demon shuddered.

Declan looked at Alerion, who was shaking from laughter.

"I promise I'm going to pay for your therapy, sons."

"There is no therapy on this earth that can undo what my mind's eye has just shown me." Dre furiously rubbed at his eyes.

"Uh, I guess it's too late to maybe discuss the trial against the Knave of Hearts?" Sammy tried to steer the discussion back to the book, a noble intention, even if completely futile. Once they got this far off-topic, there was no going back. Declan blamed it on the witches, who were remarkably dirty minded for two old women. And of course, Emilia's prudishness. These two opposing points never failed to create a great deal of friction. *Speaking of friction....*

Declan put his hand on Alerion's thigh. They had planned to leave the meeting early anyway. "Why don't we all go home to contemplate the trial scene and discuss it at the next meeting? Perhaps Barion and Jon can have a closer look as to how this scene was depicted in the movies?"

"What? It's just getting interesting," Mavis protested. Her cheeks were a healthy pink, and her eyes were glowing.

"I think Declan is right. None of us is in the right frame of mind to further concentrate on the topic." Amber got up, dragging Emilia with her. "Let's go home and ponder the scene."

The banshee and the vampire quickly left the bookshop after bidding their goodbye to Sammy, making all of them wonder what exactly these two were up to.

Mavis and Maribel left soon after, leaving the demons and their mates alone. Declan knew Alerion would never leave Sammy to tidy up on his own, so he caught Troy's gaze and they both got up to help collect all the cups and plates. Sammy seemed a bit disappointed, though only until Dre leaned into him and whispered something in his ear. Then he blushed furiously and couldn't clean the coffee machine fast enough.

When the book shop was ready for opening the next morning, they said their goodbyes and Alerion took them home. Mr. Fluffy Sparkle Pants was nowhere in sight, probably out hunting rats. He now did it for fun and apparently to keep his new roommates on their toes. There was nothing like looking for bits of dead rats in the kitchen early in the morning. So far, the count was Mr. Fluffy Sparkle Pants four, Declan and his mates five. Having superior senses did help, but only when they were awake enough to process what said senses were telling them.

"I loved it. Your book club meetings are fun!" Alerion was grinning from ear to ear.

"We're glad you liked it. And once we have dealt with the council and your sons start helping you with the ruling, you can partake more often." Troy pressed a soft kiss on Alerion's chest.

"Oh, yeah. I can't wait. Also, we have to read this trial scene really carefully. Sammy seemed devastated that we couldn't discuss it today. I want to make him happy."

"We will, beloved mate. Now let's go to bed. We have the council to deal with tomorrow — which is its own trial scene, come to think of it." Declan sighed.

He was torn about the whole thing. On the one hand, he was looking forward to cutting the council members off for good. Not their heads, obviously, as the Queen of Hearts wanted to do with Alice.

On the other hand, he knew this meant more work and therefore less time for them in the near future — time they should be spending with their mate, not with a bunch of shifters who basically just wanted to be left alone anyway. Unfortunately, Declan knew only too well what happened when people thought their supervision was gone. There were always some enterprising souls who took this as an invitation to test old boundaries. Even though shifters weren't as adventurous as demons, they still could get up to a lot of mischief.

He watched as Troy started taking off his T-shirt to go on where they had left off before the meeting. Perhaps this wasn't the worst idea—letting off some steam so they had a clear head tomorrow. Alerion was obviously very much on board, and who was Declan to rain on his mates' parade? With a smile, he followed his men to the bedroom.

# Chapter Fifteen

The next morning brought the severed head of a rat under the table in the kitchen — Mr. Fluffy Sparkle Pants seemed to have channeled the Queen of Hearts — as well as its gall bladder in the hall, where Troy had almost stepped on it. It was only thanks to Alerion's quick reflexes that he didn't have to scrape innards from the bare soles of his feet. Mr. Fluffy Sparkle Pants looked decidedly disappointed, which in turn lifted Troy's mood.

Breakfast consisted of lots of coffee and bacon eaten directly from the pan. They all were tense, because no matter how carefully they had planned the downfall of the council, there were still things that could go wrong. And despite being uber alphas, neither Declan nor Troy made a habit of destroying people's lives, which, in a sense, had led to this situation. If they had been more forceful, they could have gotten rid of the council a long time ago or tried to bend its members to their will — another thing Troy abhorred. Exerting dominance just because some mangy wolf god had given it to them in an attempt to force the world under his will? Not Troy's idea of talent well used.

After a quick shower, they dressed in slacks and shirts, wanting to exude a sense of professionalism but not so much as to make the council think they were taking them too seriously. It was a thin line to walk, especially since they all three left the top buttons of their shirts open. Declan and Troy to give a visible statement whose mates they were — Troy would never tire of seeing the intricate swirls announcing he was mate of Alerion and Declan — and Alerion to show some scales, just to remind people how very important it was to stay civil when dealing with a demon. Troy hoped the subtle mixture of understated business attire and veiled threat would be enough to avoid unpleasantness, though with the council it was always hard to tell. One last glance into the mirror and Alerion opened space and time for their travel to New York.

They had opted to pop directly into the large assembly hall where the council members liked to speak their verdicts and hold court. It was built to intimidate, seven uncomfortable looking chairs with impossibly high backs, placed on a dais, of course, and put in a semicircle. The room was empty. The council members clearly hadn't expected them to go directly to the heart of their power. With a mischievous grin, Troy went for the seat in the middle, knowing it was Elder Simarl's chair.

"What do you think? Would I look good as the head of the council?" He let himself drop into the seat, only to get back up immediately. The chairs were even more uncomfortable than they looked. "Damn. Now I know why they always look so constipated. I would, too, if I had to sit on a chair like this for any length of time."

"How about we just get rid of them? Before they come barging in." Declan pointed at the offending pieces of furniture.

"It would be my pleasure." Alerion made another slicing motion and grabbed the chair closest to him. With a broad grin, he tossed the chair through the black rip. Troy thought he heard a crackling sound.

"Where are they going?" he asked while aiming at the opening with the chair he'd just sat on.

"Oh, a nice little hell dimension that's currently in its hot phase. These things'll burn so completely there won't even be ashes left." Alerion hefted the next two chairs while Declan got the two at the right side of the semi-circle. With only one chair left, Troy took the honor of ridding the room of it. The moment the chair's back vanished inside the rip, the doors to the assembly hall were tossed open so forcefully that they creaked in their hinges. Only a very angry shifter could exert that much force on doors so sturdy.

"What is going on here?" Elder Simarl entered the room, closely followed by the other six members of the council, as well as some guards. The elders all looked furious, while the guards eyed Alerion warily. Thanks to the scales, his demonic nature was blatantly obvious, even for the densest people, and Troy hoped very much the guards would realize that following the orders of the council against Alerion would be suicide.

Declan turned to the huffing group with a broad smile on his lips, showing more fang than a smile required. "We're ridding you of these highly uncomfortable chairs and saving you some serious back pain. I can't understand how you could stand to sit on these. You can thank us now."

For a brief moment Troy thought Elder Simarl would faint from indignation right on the spot. He didn't and instead puffed up his chest in a clear attempt to intimidate.

"This is a sacred place! You have no right changing anything in here. This is where we decide on the fate of the shifter world!"

The other elders nodded vehemently, though refrained from voicing their anger. Whether out of fear of them or simply because Simarl was their designated speaker, Troy couldn't tell — and he didn't care, either. He and Declan had investigated each of the elders and knew they all were cut from the same cloth — conservative, power-hungry, greedy, not really interested in the common good, just their own gain. In short, unfit to rule.

"Well, we're here to change a lot of things, starting with this so-called *sacred* place." Declan stepped down from the dais. Alerion followed him, and Troy flanked him on the right. He had no problem letting his mate take the lead.

"Now, what do you have to say for yourself about the kidnapping of Phyllis and Lilly? And the blackmail of Tino and Jules?"

Elder Simarl crossed his arms in front of his chest, a gesture the other elders mimicked. Robbed of their regal chairs, they looked lost and far less confident than the last time Troy and Declan had met the group. He couldn't say he felt sorry for them.

"Well, whatever they have told you, it's clearly lies. What do you expect from three omegas, one of them a child, and a woman who is raising three children alone because her mate couldn't stand to be with her?" Simarl scoffed.

Troy filed the information about Phyllis away for later. If she really was alone with three children—though he didn't know if Tino was one of them or wasn't counted because he was already old enough to go to university—she'd need help, and they would see to it that she got it. Already the work was piling up.

"So you didn't only kidnap a child but also a single mother without any regard for her poor children? I have to say, I like the sound of this less and less." Declan's voice was edging into a snarl while Alerion's scales started rippling, indicating he would be growing into his demon form soon.

The elders seemed to realize that things were getting dicey because they subtly built more distance between them and Simarl, who obviously didn't notice. "What poor children? She should have kept her legs closed. As for the omegas? Everybody knows that's the only thing they're good for."

"Jules is studying law, and Tino is a business major. I'd say they are good for a lot more than what you're indicating." Declan's patience was running thin. Troy could see it in the tense set of his mate's shoulders and twitch in his jaw.

"Even if that were true, which I doubt, because who has ever heard of an omega ever achieving anything besides popping out pups, they have to obey the council. They were sent to have your pups, and as they have clearly failed, we will punish them accordingly."

There was so much wrong in that speech that Troy didn't even know where to start. It was almost as if it was Fenris talking through the elder—a frightening image if there ever was one. Troy wasn't sure how far Fenris' reach was, though since the elder wasn't frothing yet, he assumed the man simply was that narrow minded and backward.

Declan had the same feelings, because he went right for the throat, figuratively speaking. Troy was glad for it, because he was starting to feel itchy from all the vileness he could sense coming from the council.

"Well, this is where we have a great difference of opinion, which is why we are going to part ways." Declan looked at Simarl, waiting for a reaction.

"You're going to leave your own people behind, again?" Clearly the elder was too dense to understand. Declan blew on the nails of his right hand.

"No, *you* are going to leave your people behind. You're fired...all of you."

It took a few moments for the words to sink in. Then the elders all started talking at once.

"You can't..."

"That's impossible, you need us!"

"How dare you! Without us, everything will collapse."

"This is unheard of —"

Declan lifted a hand. "Silence." He infused the word with his uber alpha power, which had the entire council shutting up as if somebody had slapped a hand over their mouths.

*We should have done this sooner*, Troy thought.

"The decision has been made." Declan shook his head in warning when Simarl opened his mouth. The elder shut it with an audible *click* of his teeth. "We have watched you for some time, and as long as you left us alone, we didn't meddle in your affairs, either, which, in hindsight, was probably a mistake — one we're going to undo now. As of this moment, the council is officially disbanded until we appoint new members to rule the shifter world in our stead."

Declan turned to the guards, who had stood like statues at the doors. "Please inform everybody of our decision. Until we have found new representatives, all grievances are to be run by me and my mates. We will give you the phone numbers under which you can reach us. All trials are pending until we had a chance to look at the laws and change them where we find them lacking."

The guards looked from Troy and his mates to the council. Slowly, a smile appeared on the face of the captain—or so Troy assumed, because he had a different uniform than the rest. "We will do so, Alphas. Anything else?"

"For the moment, no. We'll need your contact information and your name, though." Declan nodded at the man.

"I'm Lucas. You can count on the guard, Alphas."

"Thank you, Lucas. We appreciate it."

"What?" Elder Simarl finally had found his voice again, much to Troy's dismay. The other elders didn't look too happy, either. Time to deal the final blow to get them off their backs. Declan winked at his mates. Troy could sense how much his mate was enjoying this after Elder Simarl had shown how little regard he had for others.

"If I were you, Elders, I'd leave this be and hurry home. I believe you'll find your financial affairs in disarray."

"What do you mean by that?" It was a woman who snapped at them, completely forgetting that she was facing her uber alphas and the demon king. Troy thought her name was Lucretia, but he wasn't sure.

"We took the liberty of cutting off your incomes. It's inconvenient for you but a lot less bloody than what shifter law dictates should happen to wolves not obeying their alphas. As of this moment, you are all more or less ruined, though we have no doubt you're going to rebuild your fortunes if you put enough effort in it. After all, you're *'alphas and above all other shifters'*. Your words, not mine. This should be child's play for you." Declan turned first to Troy then to Alerion. "Do you have anything to add, beloved mates?"

Alerion shrugged. Troy took Declan's hand and kissed it. "No. You said it perfectly, mate of ours."

"Then we're leaving. We'll be back tomorrow to establish a new council, and we expect you lot to be gone by then. Of course, you can collect personal items from your offices." Declan gave the stunned council members a lazy salute before he turned to Lucas, who was still standing at the door. Two of his fellow guards were gone, no doubt delivering the news to all the shifters working at the office. "Lucas, you're in charge till tomorrow. We're going to make an official announcement where we will also introduce the new council. Do you think you can steer this ship until then?"

Lucas shrugged. "This is not a ship. It's a tanker. It's probably going to take until you come back to even register that we're going in a new direction."

Troy sniggered. "A man with a way of words. I like you, Lucas."

The guard bowed. "I do my very best."

And with that, Alerion opened a rift again and they left the council members and the office behind to step back into the soothing silence of their home.

Until Mr. Fluffy Sparkle Pants appeared out of nowhere, yowling in that deep register that meant he'd just killed something. Troy scented the air and almost gagged.

"Whatever it is he caught this time, I'm not going to clean it up."

# Chapter Sixteen

They were snuggled up in bed after a lazy round of bathtub sex, which was becoming one of Alerion's favorite places in the apartment, right after the spacious bed, of course. He hated having to disturb the tranquility of the moment. All possible deities knew they really needed it, but there were things to be discussed and since he didn't know when the next demon emergency would be taking place, he wanted it over with to enjoy his mates again.

"Who are you going to name as the new council? I was under the impression you didn't really know who you could ask." When he saw how his mates' faces were falling, Alerion hastened to reassure them. Even though they were uber alphas and successful businessmen, they were remarkably insecure when it came to their decisions concerning the shifter world — probably because it was a responsibility they had gladly ignored until recently. "You did great back at the office. Cutting the elders off like you did was impressive. Even leaving after giving your orders was a good move. It showed that you know they will be carried out. Still, you need to give them somebody who they can rely on."

"Why do I get the impression you're going to present us with possible choices, my beloved mate?" Troy was rolling over onto his back, grinning broadly while sneaking a glance at Alerion from the side.

"Because even though our mating hasn't been that long, you're already remarkably in tune with how I think?"

"Good guess!" Troy snickered then drew in a sharp breath when Alerion's hand landed on his belly.

"We would love to hear your words of wisdom." Declan was poised on his elbow, his intense blue eyes alive with mirth.

"I'm wise enough to hear sarcasm, you know." Alerion huffed, feigning annoyance.

"Just to lighten things up," Declan hurried to say. "And if you're really angry, you can punish me later."

The sudden flare in pheromones in the air made it known how very much all three of them could get on board with this idea.

"Uh, what were we talking about?" Alerion's mind was filled with images of him having Declan over his lap, his delicious ass exposed and red from the slaps he had gotten, while Troy held their mate's hands to keep him from shielding the jiggling globes.

"About possible candidates for the council," Troy helped.

"Ah, yes, thank you." Alerion cleared his throat with the vain hope to clear his mind as well. "It was something you said, about Tino and Jules being good for a lot more than just sex. I had the impression these two young men are very capable. You could probably do a lot worse than them for the council."

For a moment there was silence, and Alerion started doubting if he had read the situation right. When both his mates started giggling like mad, he didn't know what to make of it. Declan was the first to regain his speech.

"You, King of all Demons, are a *genius*!" He sat up and tackled Alerion, planting kisses all over his face while Troy started stroking his thighs. "Tino and Jules surely are capable. They have the spine to take this challenge, and, best of all, they're omegas. By appointing them, we not only get knowledgeable representatives, but we can also start changing some of those stupid, ingrained misconceptions shifter society has about omegas. It's almost too perfect to be true."

Alerion could see the allure, though he had to admit he hadn't thought of this from the omega angle. "Well, they still have to agree."

Declan cocked his head. "You think they won't?"

"I'm not an expert on shifters, mind you, but what I could read from their body language, I think they're going to jump at the chance, especially if it comes with a healthy check. You'll probably have to help in the beginning, until they both have their degrees, but I understand that is a matter of months? And they can hire other shifters to complete the ranks of the council."

Troy stopped stroking Alerion's thighs and glanced at the clock on the nightstand. It was only ten in the evening. "Then I guess we'd better give them a call, telling them they have a job and need to be available tomorrow after lunch."

"Perhaps it's better to ask them if they want a job and to be ready in the early afternoon?" Alerion cautioned.

Troy's shoulders slumped a bit. "You're right. Just because we want to free our time for you doesn't mean we can burden others against their will."

"Now I feel bad for even mentioning it."

Declan gave Alerion a kiss on his lips. "You were right to do so. It's also right for you to know why we are so eager to redistribute responsibilities."

Alerion could hear an undertone of something a little more sinister than just wanting to be with their mate, and he decided to address it.

"Just because I have been king to my people for so long doesn't mean I can't understand why you don't want to be. On the contrary, I know only too well how tiresome it can be, and considering how leadership has been thrust at you, I can see no fault in trying to rid yourself of it. I admire you for stepping up and acknowledging your role, even though you don't want it. Also, and this is my very humble opinion as leader of a people who will probably never be able to govern themselves through any concept resembling a democracy, I think it's a good thing you let your people learn how to get by without an absolute power governing them. It's a bit like the Roman emperors of old, who stepped up when the republic needed them, only to relinquish their power once the problem had been dealt with."

Both his mates bent forward to plant a kiss on each of his cheeks. "Thank you," they said in unison, expressing with two words what even a three-hour speech wouldn't have been able to convey.

Gratitude, love, admiration, respect.

Troy and Declan deserved it all, as well, because they both had dared at a young age to defy the will of a god and thus changed the course of fate. Alerion was sure the Fates couldn't have made them mates if there hadn't been the seed of rebellion against Fenris and an underlying penchant for love, not violence, deep in their hearts. It was, of course, only speculation, because not even he ever talked to the Fates, but Alerion hadn't gotten where he was today, knowing what he did, by being ignorant. He knew to trust his gut, and his gut told him that Declan and Troy were a chance the Fates had granted the shifter world.

"Fine... Let's see if we can get Tino and Jules to work for us." Troy interrupted Alerion's musings.

Taking his cell from the nightstand, he was already calling Sammy.

"Yeah, hello, Sammy. Sorry to disturb you so late, but is there a chance for us to talk to Tino or Jules?" A pause. "They're both there? What a lucky coincidence."... "Yes, please give them your cell. It's nothing bad, but we just had an idea."... "Is it good? Please, you know us!"... "What does that mean, that's why? Our ideas are brilliant!"... "Well, yes, Vegas might have been a bit less brilliant."... "No, Zurich was great. I stand by that."... "I'm not sure I still like you, Sammy. How do you even remember all this?"... "You have a diary?"... "That's sweet, yes, and no, I'm not mocking him, Dre. Declan and I have thought about having one as well, but we never had the time and... Anyway, why would you write such things down, Sammy? To embarrass your friends?"... "For birthdays and special occasions? Okay, that's actually a good idea."... "Yes."... "No, as I said, it's nothing bad, and they have every right to say no."... "Yes, I'm going to stress that."... "Yes, thank you, Sammy and a good night to you, too!"

Troy flashed them a crooked smile while shrugging. Then he started grinning.

"Tino, Jules, how are you? Is it okay if I put you on speaker for Declan and Alerion to hear? We have a proposal for you."

\* \* \* \*

"I have to say, they drive a hard bargain." Alerion leaned back on the bed while Troy put his cell back on the nightstand, looking exhausted. Tino and Jules hadn't been averse to the idea of becoming part of the shifter government, but they had very clear ideas about what they wanted and how they wanted it. Negotiating with them had taken over two hours.

Alerion had been silent most of the time, only giving his opinion once or twice when he had the feeling his mates were getting stuck. All in all, the discussion had shown that neither Tino nor Jules would be easily taken advantage of, and with the backing of their uber alphas, they should be going a long way. Alerion also didn't get the impression they would ever suffer silently should they not be happy with something, which was good. It was nice if his mates had people they could delegate to, but they still needed to be kept in the loop, which Tino and Jules would surely do. Now, to get his mates back to bed and to sleep without giving in to temptation, which was riding him hard.

As it turned out, his mates were just as bad at withstanding their combined sexual lure, which led to an interesting, athletic night, only interrupted once by their furry roommate.

\* \* \* \*

"Why didn't we stop after the second round?" Declan was staring into his cup of coffee with a miserable expression. It was almost time to pick up Tino and Jules, and because they still had a business to run, the two alphas had needed to get up in the morning. Out of solidarity, Alerion had joined them, even though he was regretting it the whole time.

Declan was *not* a morning person.

Troy was a bit better, though not by much, and Mr. Fluffy Sparkle Pants had contributed to the overall shitty morning by first getting into the drawer where his treats were kept and eating half of them, only to vomit them all up on the carpet in the living room, just a few inches from the hardwood floor that could have been cleaned so much easier. Because both his mates had been like zombies and preparing for a video call, it had fallen to Alerion to clean up the mess, just like he had taken care of the unidentifiable prey their tom had brought the other night.

Never had Alerion been happier about his talent to open space and time. All it took was a quick swipe directly above the offending sludge on the ground, not too wide, to avoid having the entire carpet sucked into the vacuum dimension he had come across by chance some eight hundred years ago, and the mess was gone — at least mostly. He still had to shampoo the place where the contents of Mr. Fluffy Sparkle Pants' stomach had been, but compared to picking up the still recognizable, slimy bits and pieces with wadded up kitchen paper, this was a piece of cake.

Now they were getting ready to go back to the office, and Alerion had written Sammy a text, asking him to prepare his mates' favorite drinks to hopefully wake them up a bit. He also vowed to himself not to have sex before important meetings in the future — or at least not so much sex. Then again, if asked, Alerion wouldn't have traded the previous night for some sound sleep. He only hoped their libido would still be going strong in a few thousand years.

"Come on, you two. I have it on good authority that if you get your asses in gear now, you won't leave Sammy's shop emptyhanded."

Both his mates perked up. Had they been in their wolf form, Alerion was sure they would have wagged their tails like crazy. The power of Sammy's coffee concoctions was beyond all imagination.

After Declan and Troy had gotten enough sweetened caffeine into their systems to resemble functioning members of society again, they took Tino and Jules to the office in New York. After an introduction to the assembled shifters working there, laced with some subtle threats should people not cooperate with their new bosses and taking Lucas' promise to help Tino and Jules get acquainted with everything, they left the two omegas to their own devices, promising either Alerion or one of his sons would pick them up in the evening. For the time being, Tino and Jules would commute from Beaconville via demon, until the dust had settled, and a semblance of normalcy was established. The moment they came back home, Alerion was called to see after his demons.

This time they had apparently visited a dimension with spotty gravity to replay one of the demo-levels Barion and Jon had put out on the web. It reminded Alerion that the talk with his sons was still due and that the game may not be able to be released to the general public. He already hated himself for having mentioned it to the two without them having a way to work around it.

Life could be such a bitch sometimes.

Declan and Troy agreed to invite Dre and Barion with their mates for dinner the next evening, which gave Alerion an entire day to fret about how to break the potentially bad news to them. Well, almost the entire day, because there were still two mates who needed to be sexed up and another group of demons who needed it explained for the thousandth time how bad it was for the fragile minds of humans to see a demon in their full scaly glory, let alone *naked*.

# Chapter Seventeen

Declan loved Troy. He really did, from the bottom of his heart, like mad. He was one third of his soul, the light in his darkness, the joy in his eyes. Also, if the bumbling idiot didn't leave the kitchen right *now*, he would not be responsible for his actions.

"How many times have I told you that Sammy doesn't like onions in his potato salad? Did you listen? No, you went ahead and dumped the entire bowl in that I chopped. Now what are we supposed to give Sammy as a side dish for his grilled cheese?" Declan glared at Troy, who had the decency to look chagrined.

"I thought you'd forgotten to put them in." He waved the now-empty bowl that had contained the chopped onions in the air.

Declan groaned. Normally he didn't mind Troy's clumsiness in the kitchen. Normally, it was a fun way of getting apology blow jobs out of him. Normally, he didn't cook for his newest mate's two sons and their partners, who always dished up the most delicious food because they could simply hop around the world and get it fresh from the source.

Declan was a decent cook, nobody starved on his watch and at least he didn't cheat when he cooked for his guests. He thought of the tales about Barion's adventures in the kitchen and decided that sometimes cheating was preferable to having to build a new house. But Dre could cook. The red idiot just loved to impress his mate with gourmet food from all over the world. And Sammy was shamelessly enabling him by loving it.

"What made you think anything happening in this kitchen isn't on purpose?"

"Is that a trick question?" Troy put the bowl down, carefully eyeing Declan.

"No, babe, I'm sorry." Declan put the spatula he had used to clear the air with forceful motions on the kitchen counter. "This is just the first time we're entertaining Alerion's family here. I'm a little nervous."

Troy huffed. The idiot huffed! In that moment, it was crystal clear to Declan that he was definitely the brains in this operation if his gorgeous — though obviously thick — mate couldn't see the severity of the situation.

On the floor, Mr. Fluffy Sparkle Pants meowed hopefully. So far he had managed to shame both of them into giving him half an escalope from the cutting board where Declan had seasoned and crumbed the meat. At least somebody was having a good afternoon.

"What is there to be nervous about? We've known Sammy and Jon for *ages,* and I'm not sure how often we've eaten with the four of them. It's not like we're meeting strangers."

"I know that, Troy. It's the context! Don't you get it? I'm not cooking for the slightly — okay, make that absolutely—scatterbrained head of our book club and our zombie-computer geek friend. I'm also not cooking for the two demons who have recently joined our merry band of avid readers. I'm cooking for our *sons*! For the first time." There, now Troy had to understand.

"It really bothers you, huh?"

"Is that all you have to say?" Declan couldn't believe it. This was the man he shared his mate, body, home and business with. How had he never realized how dumb Troy could be?

"Yes, that's all I have to say, because I think you're having a meltdown for no reason at all, and I don't know how to stop it without dragging you to the bedroom and fucking your brain out so that it can have some rest." Troy eyed him with a speculative gleam in his eyes. The bastard was seriously considering it.

"No, you can't fuck my brain out, as tempting as the offer is. They're going to be here in less than thirty minutes, and I'm not done with preparations. What you can do is find out how to get the onions back out of the potato salad—or how to get some of the potatoes out."

Troy eyed the clay bowl with the lively flower pattern they had brought home from a trip to Italy. "You know him. He'll be able to tell they had contact with the gangsta veggie. Plus, I do get some Cinderella vibes here, and we both know my singing voice is more likely to attract those rats Mr. Fluffy Sparkle Pants keeps bringing home than some helpful birds."

Sadly, both statements were the naked truth. As adventurous as Sammy was when it came to food, onions were simply not acceptable. He had a sixth sense for them, and since they had met him, nobody had managed to sneak them past him in a dish, though it hadn't been for lack of trying.

Declan looked at the bowl, at the escalopes, to the pans he had already put the butter in, back to the bowl where the offending solanum was glistening against the rich yellow of the russets.

"I might have an idea." Troy got his cell.

"What are you doing?"

Troy grinned. "Texting Dre."

"Are you crazy? We said we would cook! They're invited. Guests don't bring their own food!"

"Family does, especially when said family can impress their mate by bringing a completely onion free potato salad from Bavaria, freshly made by one of Dre's many contacts. You know him. He will be delighted to show off in front of Sammy. And you won't have to stress out over how to cook fresh potatoes within thirty, no, make that twenty minutes. Win-win."

Declan wasn't happy, but Troy had a point. Family was supposed to stick together, right? "Fine. Let Dre have his moment of glory. I'm frying the meat." He turned toward the stove, just in time to see an orange shadow sneaking off with an entire escalope. "*You son of a bitch!*" Declan felt his fangs lengthening.

"I told you the Fluffy Sparkle Pants was just a ruse!" Troy made no move to follow the feline thief. They couldn't serve the bounty to their guests anymore, and starting a hunt would have only served to embolden the tom further. In moments like these, Declan seriously wondered why they ever thought giving Alerion a street cat would be a good idea. *It must have been a moment of delusion*, he decided, brought on by the happy mating pheromones that had been flooding their brains.

With a deep sigh that couldn't quite express the heaviness Declan felt settling on his shoulders, he fired up the stove.

* * * *

"This was simply delicious." Sammy leaned back in his chair, beaming at both his mate and Declan. "You're an incredible cook, Declan. And you, my mate, are the best buyer of potato salad in the whole world."

Dre visibly puffed up. With any other person, Declan would have been sure they were making fun of Dre. Sammy meant every word he said. The poor, naïve boy truly thought hopping over to Bavaria and getting some food was a feat of greatness.

"I'm not so sure about Dre's prowess, but the food was amazing, Declan." Barion, always the younger sibling, had no problem taking his brother down a few notches. Dre's eyes narrowed. The two brothers had been surprisingly peaceful during dinner, perhaps because Alerion had looked so tired when he had come back from his latest mission. Before they could break this streak, Declan got up to collect the dishes.

"Wait till you see the pie I made for dessert."

"There will be pie?" Jon perked up. The zombie had a bit of a sweet tooth.

"Yes. Apple crumble." Declan had the recipe from Mavis and Maribel. It annoyed him that he still wasn't able to reproduce it exactly like they did, but it was more than decent.

After Sammy and Jon had moaned over the pie, Alerion cleared his throat. Their demon mate was clearly reluctant to broach the subject. They both put a hand on Alerion's thighs, silently encouraging him.

"There is something I'd like to discuss with you…all of you." Alerion looked at his four sons. Dre and Barion shared a quick glance, while Sammy leaned forward. Jon simply nodded. He was fully engaged in eating his third slice of pie. Paranormal metabolism was such a wonderful thing.

"Of course. We are always there for you, Dad!" Sammy beamed happily.

"Well, you might not be so eager once you know what I'm going to propose."

"If you keep dancing around the subject, you won't find out." Dre had his hand on Sammy's nape, lazily stroking the line where hair turned to bare skin.

Alerion squirmed a bit. Declan glanced at Troy, silently asking if they should intervene. Troy cocked his head slightly, which meant they should give their mate a few more minutes—or he was wondering what Declan was asking. It was hard to tell. Their mate drew a deep breath.

"I've talked to my beloved mates, seeing as they have found reliable representatives to share the burden of leadership with them, even though it's still fairly new, but it looks promising, and because I want to spend more time with them, which you surely can understand, I wanted to ask if you thought it possible to become my helpers?"

The sentence was a bit winded, but it was finally out, which was the only thing that counted.

"Of course we're going to help. Won't we, Dre, beloved?" Sammy fluttered his lashes at Dre, who caved immediately.

"*Mo grah thu*, you know we do." Then he looked up at his father. "What exactly do you have in mind?"

Instead of answering, Alerion turned to Barion and Jon, who hadn't said anything yet. Both of them nodded with a smile. "I think it's actually a great idea. We've been worried about your workload," Jon commented.

"Well, concerning my workload... There's a reason our demons have gotten so creative." Alerion lowered his gaze. "I can't find the words to express how sorry I am, but Barion, Jon, *Demon Wars* may not be able to go public. Demons everywhere have seen your demo videos and are now trying to reenact them. They love your work."

For a moment, it was so silent that they could hear the soft rustling as yet another cat toy died a silent death under Mr. Fluffy Sparkle Pants' claws.

"Oh," was all Jon said. Barion just stared at his father.

"You can't!" Sammy shoved his plate forward. "Jon and Barion have worked so hard to set this whole game up. People are so excited for it!"

"Which apparently is the problem, *mo grah thu*." Dre patted his younger brother's back in a conciliatory way. As much as the two fought all the time, when push came to shove, they were always there for each other. "When demons get excited, things can get out of hand quickly. You know this."

Sammy shook his head vehemently, as if denying the truth would make it somehow go away. Given the suddenly determined gleam in Dre's eyes, his tactic might be successful. Dre hated seeing his mate upset. To be honest, Declan and Troy hated seeing Sammy upset as well, as did Alerion. Barion and Jon were upset right along with Sammy, unable to think at all. They all stared at the table for some time, trying to find a solution to this problem without having to shut the game down before it even came out.

Then all of a sudden Sammy thumped the table so hard the plates did a little jump. Sammy winced and started shaking his hands until Dre took them at the wrists to blow on the palms.

"I assume your abuse of our poor dinner table means you had an idea?" Declan felt a weak tug at the corners of his mouth. Humans could be so adorable. Well, former humans. Though Sammy had always been adorable. So yes, humans *and* former humans.

"Yes! The best." Sammy's eyes sparkled happily. "I think it will take care of *all* our problems at once!" He turned to Alerion. "Dad, some days ago, I think you mentioned something about a group of demons who go to renaissance fairs?"

Alerion nodded slowly.

"I assume they are using Jon's and Barion's video game as their inspiration?"

"Yes, among other sources." Alerion looked at his youngest son and son-in-law. "The humans love the show."

"Which makes my solution so perfect." Sammy had gotten up from his chair, too excited to stay seated. "Why don't we make little YouTube videos with scenes from *Demon Wars*?"

It was official. Sammy had lost his ever-loving mind, most possibly fucked out by his demon mate. What else could be the reason for such an outrageously dumb suggestion? Declan shook his head, glanced at Troy and Alerion, who were clearly trying to find a diplomatic response to shut down Sammy's so-called idea.

"Excuse me, Sammy. I just heard you want to do the equivalent of feeding a bunch of hyped-up five-year-olds a ton of sugar." Declan softened his blow with a smile he hoped was friendly and open and not of the stay-calm-the-nice-people-in-white-are-on-their-way variety. Sammy furrowed his brows as if he hadn't thought of that aspect yet.

*Adorable, but also thick as a field of lard*, Declan thought, not without affection.

"No. Yes. In a way. Hear me out. I promise, the idea *is* perfect." Like a wolverine with a bit of meat, Sammy wasn't willing to let go of his idea.

"That's not the description I was thinking of," Declan cut in to snip any hope on Sammy's side in the bud. "More like dangerous. Reckless, surely. Insane, definitely."

Sammy's lower lip started to tremble. Dre's fangs grew out. Declan hurried to mime zipping his lips, indicating he would be listening.

"Now, *mo grah thu*, go on with your idea, which I'm sure is far greater than Declan can imagine." The warning was clear, and Declan wiggled a little closer to Alerion, who put an arm around him. At least Dre would have to go through his father first before he could do any harm to Declan. Sammy perked up, a bright smile on his lips.

"Think about it. Are you going to have a bunch of demons wreaking absolute havoc? Absolutely. Will you find out *after* the damage is done? No. Because we will be the ones who dictate when and where what kind of havoc will be wreaked. And any demon who goes on unauthorized solo missions is banned from the fun."

"I hate to say this, but I kind of like the idea…" Troy drummed a short, unrecognizable rhythm on the table. Sammy clapped his hands and went on.

"We tell the demons we're looking for actors to play some of the scenes from *Demon Wars*. Everybody is welcome, no weapon is too outrageous, they can fight in their true form and have as much fun as they want, as long as they follow the script. I'm sure Barion and Jon can acquire some drones and film cameras to get workable footage of the fights. Then they can cut them into little videos they can show to make people more curious about the game. And once the game is out, the videos will keep people interested. It's good advertising." Sammy was panting as if he'd run a marathon, which, in a certain way, he had. After his initial — and totally justified — doubts, the sheer beauty of Sammy's idea blinded Declan a bit.

"Sammy, I take back everything I said and apologize for ever doubting you. You're a genius. Barion and Jon can get their game out." Declan started counting the points on his right hand. "By saying only demons who behave on earth are allowed to play, we keep them on a tight leash. By scripting it, we can take turns supervising them when they play, and even if they go off-script, it should still make for great images. It's wonderful advertisement, and if we do it right, this could even be an additional source of income. When the equipment allows it, we can even film in other dimensions where the demons can let loose completely without upsetting anybody, and nobody will suspect a thing because CGI these days is just that good. Well done, Sammy!" Declan got up to hug the young man.

Sammy's smile was so broad, it almost reached his ears. "I told you it was a good idea."

Huge, black-scaled arms wound around them both. Alerion's joy was evident in his voice. "Thank you, Sammy. I'm so glad Barion and Jon can keep *Demon Wars*."

Speaking of which — Declan extracted himself from the snuggle pile. Troy and Dre were only too happy to take his place.

"What do you two think? You've been awfully quiet." Declan looked at Barion and Jon.

The zombie was clutching his fork like a lifeline, and Barion had a glazed-over look, as if somebody had hit him with a brick...several times. Jon put the fork down.

"I have to admit I've just gotten over the shock that our game was the reason Dad had so much work recently."

"*Part* of the reason," Alerion hastened to correct. "They've been restless before. Your wonderful game simply channeled their energies." Which sounded a lot better than saying it caused them to set fire to a warehouse district and play war at purely human events. "So what do you think? Is it a good idea?"

"Well, from our point of view, definitely," Barion said. "The question is will we be able to keep things... well, organized is probably the wrong word, as is civil....in a way that nobody gets hurt or banished?"

Alerion let Sammy go but kept his arm around Troy, looking first at him then at Declan. They both nodded.

Alerion squared his shoulders. "Yes. There might be some bumps in the road, but they'll be there no matter what we do. It's the nature of the beast — or demon, so to speak. I propose we start by asking Allienna, the demoness who leads the renaissance fair squad, to help us. And the first few fights should be in another dimension, just to be on the safe side. If my demons show they can behave, we can move on to locations here on Earth."

"Uh, this is going to be so much fun! Jon, can I help with the scripts? I've always wanted to dabble in filming, and I have some film scripts in my collection. Great classics, too, like *The Untouchables* and *Jaws*. And, of course, *The First Wives Club*." Sammy was like an eager puppy dropping balls in front of Jon. The zombie took Sammy's hands in his.

"Your help is always welcome. You know that."

"Wonderful." Dre rubbed his hands. "How quickly do you think you can come up with the first two or three scripts?"

Barion and Jon shared a look. "Give us four days. We should be able to put something together by then, don't you think so, *iubit*?"

Jon nodded.

"I will summon Allienna and tell her about our idea. Is there anything we're going to need?" Alerion looked around.

Barion shook his head. "Not off the top of my head. We don't need a make-up artist or CGI, just drones and cameras. Everybody hopefully brings their own weapons, and if anybody gets hungry, they can always go hunting. No big deal."

"Then it's decided. Barion, Jon, you tell us when we have to be where. I don't know about you, but I want to be at the first film set." Troy rubbed his hands like a third-class villain. Declan didn't hesitate to give his consent, as did the others.

Apart from having to clean up all the stuffing from the cat toy Mr. Fluffy Sparkle Pants had shredded, the evening had been a success.

# Chapter Eighteen

"I really think I should have both my Warhammer *and* my sword. Don't I look way cooler like this?" The demon struck a pose, lifting the hammer high over his head while pointing the sword forward to fend off an invisible enemy. The corners of his enormous axe were peeking out from where his emerald-green wings narrowed into his back.

"I don't know, Shell'rar. To me it seems a bit much," Allienna responded, hefting her own double-headed axe in her hand, the tips of her claws protruding around the handle like deadly spikes from a collar. The string of blades she had attached to the edges of her wings clinked softly.

The demons had jumped at the chance to star in the videos Barion and Jon were filming. The only problem so far was taming their creative input to keep them from tipping over. Troy had never thought it possible, but there was such a thing as too many weapons on a demon, and they had already had to help three demons and two demonesses up, who'd all been on their backs like dung beetles after their ball had become too big. It was kind of funny, really, even though Troy had done his best not to laugh out loud.

The demons were taking their new job of helping Barion and Jon promote *Demon Wars* very seriously. Hence the discussion about the right number of weapons for the next scene where a playful little encounter between two groups would lead to the discovery of a whole new level.

For this purpose, they had gone to a hell dimension, which was currently in a state where the temperatures were a cozy sixty-eight Fahrenheit and the landscape offered countless little hills and valleys where enthusiastic fighting was made more interesting by loose rocks and sliding rubble. This dimension also had spots where enterprising demons could go from one place to another via some kind of highspeed tunnel, which would lead to the discovery of the new level in the dimension with the gigantic rats, where the tunnels didn't actually lead — but that was artistic freedom for you.

Some carefully conducted experiments had shown that GoPro cameras could withstand the strain of travelling several hundred miles within a heartbeat, and the material they had from demons using several of the spots multiple times was a lot better than anything Hollywood had produced so far.

"Do you think we should wear these metal cages in front of our breasts?" It was a bright orange demoness with an impressive set of curled horns asking the question. Troy looked her over. She was in full demon form, meaning everything was covered in scales. Her breasts were, like those of all demonesses, not any bigger than the pecs of the demons. It made sense. Troy didn't even want to begin to imagine how fighting with two big sacks of meat on his front would go.

"We would need to practice first." Allienna stepped next to Troy, the sword Shell'rar had been swinging in her hand. It seemed she had won that argument. "I also think we shouldn't give humans the impression that having these things is in any way desirable." She made a face. "I still don't understand why all the female warriors on earth seem to have such big ones."

And that had been a long, very uncomfortable discussion Troy really wanted to forget. Say about demons what you wanted, but they had true gender equality. Females and males alike had been puzzled as to why the female fantasy warriors humans imagined had to look like high-performance cows.

"If I had that much meat on my front, I would rip it off."

"If they insist on keeping it, why don't they at least cover it for protection? One swing with a sword and that's *it*."

"Who would want to fight with that?"

"There's no way she can swing a sword with those balls in the way."

"Not very efficient."

Those were only a few of the comments the demons had made when Serpamon, one of the renaissance fair performers, had shown them a few games they had used as inspiration for their fighting demonstrations.

Alerion had tried, very briefly, to explain about the peculiarities of human sexism and given up quickly, just saying humans were weird and this was another example why they had to be treated with the utmost care, because clearly, they had no clue about the realities of life. Much to Troy's surprise, the demons had been fine with this explanation, thinking it was way more important what weapons would make the biggest impression.

"Allienna, there you are!" Sammy came running, Dre hot on his heels. He wasn't very happy about his mate's presence on set, mostly because other dimensions could be dangerous, but Sammy was so invested in the whole idea, not letting him be there for the first day of filming would have been plain cruel. He had promised Dre not to go to the rat dimension, mostly because he still had his shop to run. Milo was busy with school and working for Quirion, which left him little time to help Sammy. His mother would have her surgery soon, and in order to take a week off to help her, the boy tried to put in his hours in advance. It was insane, making Troy wonder when Milo would crack.

"We're ready for the first fight." Sammy waved excitedly.

Allienna hefted her battle axe and held the sword out to Troy, who took it automatically, thanking the gods for uber werewolf strength, because otherwise he would have made a fool of himself. He watched as the two demonesses followed Sammy and Dre to the spot where the first fight would start, strictly choreographed to get the best shots. As Troy understood it, there would be some freestyle fighting later, with GoPro cams attached to the demons involved. He spotted Alerion in the midst of it all, smiling happily, because for once he wasn't admonishing his demons. Only now when he didn't have to do it did they all realize how much it had weighed on him.

"What are you doing here, looking all gloomy, mate of mine?" Declan stepped behind Troy, slinging his arms around his middle and pressing a kiss to his nape.

With a satisfied sigh, Troy leaned against the comforting weight of his mate.

"Contemplating how well things are going at the moment—and waiting for the other shoe to drop."

"Pessimist. Can't you just enjoy the moment?" Declan's mocking tone wasn't as carefree as he tried to sound. He, too, was a worrywart.

"Oh, I do enjoy the moment. I'm just wondering when we'll have to step in to deal with the next catastrophe."

"I think we're pretty safe when it comes to the demons. They love this, and the possibilities are endless. With some luck, this project will have them occupied for years. And even if not, Dre and Barion are already stepping up. I think our dear mate has gained his breathing space." Declan was a bit hard to understand because he had his nose buried in Troy's nape. As wolves, scent was as important to them as bodily contact, and since they had mated with Alerion, all their scents had changed yet again.

It was now a heady mixture of berries, woods, fire and something deliciously sweet. Troy was sure the combination wasn't of earth—logical when you were mated to a demon.

"Which only leaves the council." He sighed.

Things had been surprisingly silent, with Tino and Jules hiring new people and basically overhauling the entire ruling body of the shifter world. The two omegas were exceeding their expectations, which made Troy hopeful for the future. There would still be some tough meetings where the laws of old would be re-written to fit in modern times. If the two preliminary discussions they'd had with representatives of the various shifter groups were any indication, things would get heated.

Troy hated using his uber alpha powers to just make things right for people, when it should be, in his opinion, natural to try to make everybody happy. Some of the shifter groups clung very tightly to their laws, which usually favored the strong, something Troy and Declan wanted to be a thing of the past. So yes, there was still a lot of work ahead of them.

"The *former* council has been very quiet. Emilia says they're too busy trying to salvage some of their money to make trouble for us, at least for the foreseeable future. And don't forget about the neat little curses Mavis and Maribel sent their way." Declan's voice was dripping with malicious glee.

"Remind me to never get on their bad side."

"Unless Emilia starts spouting that nonsense about *American Gods* being Neil Gaiman's most important work when clearly it is *The Graveyard Book*."

"She just can't see what's important." Troy shrugged.

Emilia's inability to rank books properly for their importance was a constant well of discussion for the entire club. Strangely enough, the others sided with her sometimes, probably to make her feel better.

Down at the filming area, Jon yelled "Action" and the demons started going at each other while Alerion was gesticulating wildly from the sidelines. Sammy was on Dre's shoulders, the safest place for him to be during the filming, as they all had agreed.

Troy had to admit the scene looked perfect, especially from their point, a little farther away from all the swooshing and swinging weapons. He wondered if Jon had somebody filming from that angle.

Behind him, Declan stepped a bit back to get his cell out. He started filming. Troy smiled. Alerion looked up to them and gave a thumbs up when he saw what Declan was doing.

Great minds *did* think alike.

# Chapter Nineteen

"Oooh, that's a really good one! I love how that orange demoness just *flips* in midair and smashes that silver demon to the ground with her battle axe. Beautiful!" Amber's tone reached almost Bansheevibrations, and Alerion was glad it was Mavis sitting next to her in front of Jon's laptop. The old witch's ears weren't as good as his or those of his mates and would therefore not take as much damage — or so he hoped. Mavis didn't seem to realize she was being blasted with a pitch that even bats would find hard to handle. She was clutching her wife's hand, pointing animatedly at the screen.

"Did you see that ass? You could bounce a whole sack of quarters off it — or crunch some Brazil nuts. We should ask if he wants to lend it to us for a bit."

"Yes, dear. I'm sure such a strapping young man is open for a little fun." Maribel had a speculative gleam in her eyes, telling Alerion she was already making plans he didn't want to know anything about. As for the 'strapping young man', Hol was roughly five hundred years old, an admittedly talented fighter and most definitely interested in anything the two witches might offer.

"I love the different angles. You did a wonderful job cutting it." Emilia sounded dreamy as she watched three demons clashing in mid-air, swords and hammers and axes clinking, all accompanied by the growls and battle cries of fifty fighters giving it their all.

Jon beamed with pride while Barion puffed his chest.

Seeing his sons so happy was the icing on Alerion's cake. With Dre's and Barion's help, and thanks to Sammy's genius idea with the videos, the demons were almost easy to handle now. There were still squabbles when the different project groups — a brilliant idea on Jon's part, keeping them occupied even when no filming was taking place — couldn't see eye to eye when it came to choreography or location, but they accepted Jon's and Barion's words as the final ruling without much backtalk. That there even were project groups was a miracle in itself. The natural size of a group of demons usually was one or two, and everything else was called a fight. Though he had to admit the demons around Allienna had shown remarkable team spirit, even before the filming. Alerion's hope that even demons could evolve was growing with each day.

"Ah, thank you, Sammy. This simply is the nectar of the gods." Troy was taking a sip of his latte, which Sammy had just handed to him over the counter in his book shop.

"You're welcome, Troy. Dad, your usual?"

Alerion nodded. "Thank you, Son."

Sammy beamed. He loved it when Alerion called him 'son', so he did it as often as possible. His mates were sauntering over to him, giving the coffee table with Jon's laptop and its excited audience a wide berth. Technically, they were here to further discuss *Alice's Adventures in Wonderland*, but when the two witches, the banshee and the vampire had heard the first videos were ready for upload, they had wanted to see them. *Alice* would have to wait until next week.

"Hey, gorgeous. What are you doing here all on your own?" Declan kissed his cheek while Troy snuggled against his side, carefully balancing his half-empty mug with coffee.

"Waiting for my mates, who have abandoned me in favor of the cheap thrill of coffee and haven't even thought of bringing my beverage."

"First, coffee isn't a cheap thrill. It's vital." Declan lifted his right index finger. "Second...uhm, we didn't bring your beverage because it would make Sammy sad if he couldn't deliver it."

"Ha!" came a huff from the counter. Clearly, Sammy's sadness knew strict boundaries.

"Fine." Declan took a sip from his drink. "We're terrible mates who had an exhausting day and have forgotten to bring you your hot chocolate." He made puppy-dog eyes, which worked remarkably well, considering he was a fearsome uber alpha. Well, to the world, he was a fearsome uber alpha. To Alerion and Troy, Declan was a ball of silken fur who couldn't say no to their resident cat.

Just yesterday Alerion had caught Declan giving out forbidden treats to the demanding feline around midnight. Mr. Fluffy Sparkle Pants had shamelessly fled the scene and left Declan to his fate, which hadn't deterred Declan from giving him another treat in the morning.

Alerion stroked his mate's head. "I know, love. I'm so proud of both of you."

"Speaking of which, tell us about the new laws." Mavis looked up from the laptop. The video was over.

Alerion put a hand on both his mates' lower backs to guide them to the sofa with the rainbow throw. Once they were all seated, Sammy came over with his hot chocolate, so it was apparently story time. Declan looked at Troy, who shrugged. Alerion knew this was his mates' way of deciding who got to talk and who could lean back and enjoy the show. So far, he hadn't found the pattern to their decision-making yet, though it seemed to be balanced. Today it was Troy's turn. He cleared his throat.

"Initially we wanted to bring the laws into modern times, as you know, but the resistance among the representatives of the shifter groups was enormous. It was quite the headache. Finally, Tino and Jules suggested annulling them all and writing completely new ones, taking into account human laws to make it easier to navigate both worlds. Boy, what a headache." Both werewolves shook their heads.

"I know. My sisters talked of great upheaval in the shifter world." Amber grinned impishly. She didn't seem to think upheaval was something bad.

"The vampires are very interested, as well. Quite a few of the younger ones are demanding the same should happen for our species." Emilia sipped her green tea. "Even though the old ones don't want to see it, change is a good thing." There was a hint of maliciousness in her voice, suggesting she enjoyed the discomfort of 'the old ones' a great deal.

"Yes, it is. It's also damn hard to implement, which I suspect is one reason why some people are so adamantly against it." Troy huffed. "Luckily, the most conservative of the bunch are still hyperventilating because we appointed two omegas as our stand-ins, which kept them from interfering too much. Anyway, the new laws are written down and ratified, including one saying that if in the future any of those laws proof unsuitable for the shifter community, they can be changed." Troy sighed.

He and Declan were very happy they had managed to include this law. They hoped it would prevent problems, like omegas technically not being allowed to go to school then work, as it had been the case in recent years. Tino and Jules were lucky they had progressive parents who hadn't wanted them to be dependent on anybody. There were many omegas who had it worse—omegas they were trying to help with the new laws. Alerion was so proud of his mates, who were stepping up to their duties now that they had realized how badly the council had abused its powers.

"Yes, change is good and so important." Mavis snuggled against Maribel. "It's nice to see it happening and even nicer to have a hand in it."

"Yes, it's all coming together nicely." Amber reached for the last red velvet muffin on the table.

"And it's not a coincidence, is it?" Alerion looked around the original members of the book club, as well as the newcomers, who were all demons.

Mavis lifted a brow. "You've caught on to it as well." It was a statement, not a question.

"I wouldn't be a good king to my people if I hadn't. Plus, it's rather obvious."

Maribel sighed. "It is. Though it took us some time to see it, probably because we were waiting for so long for the other shoe to drop."

"Can somebody tell me what you're talking about?" Sammy was snuggled against Dre's broad chest, nibbling on his own muffin. Dre gave him a loving kiss on the head.

"Well, basically they're talking about you, *mo grah thu*."

"Me?" Sammy looked at them all.

"Yes, dear." Mavis put her hand on Maribel's thigh. "Have you never wondered why there are no other paranormals in Beaconville? And why the few that are here are drawn to your bookshop?"

"Well, I thought that was just me. You know, me being a magnet for anything paranormal. And you're all really nice, and I like you a lot. Why shouldn't we spend time together?"

"Because normally, werewolves and vampires don't mix, not to mention witches and banshees or witches and vampires. As for real zombies, there aren't enough to really know it, but my bet would be, if there were more than just Jon and his Grann, they would keep to themselves as well." Amber winked at Jon. "Us sitting here, drinking tea, eating pastries, not killing each other, instead being friends? That's an anomaly, Sammy — something that shouldn't be possible."

Sammy furrowed his brows, thinking hard. He looked like an adorable baby bunny when he did that. "You told me that numerous times, and I still don't believe it. You're all so good together."

"We are. In part, all of us are here because we escaped the confines of our societies, which makes us similar, in a way." Emilia twirled one of her gorgeous chestnut curls around her fingers. "Still, I would have never considered talking to Troy and Declan or Amber or Mavis and Maribel — not to mention Jon, though I would have never met him because he never left his cellar."

The others nodded.

"Then what made you go to the book club?" Alerion looked around.

"We were drawn by a feeling of urgency. We knew we had to be here." Maribel tapped her chin thoughtfully. "Good thing, too, because these two" — she pointed at Amber and Declan — "had such warped ideas about the importance of Mary Shelley's work."

"Which we have amended by now," Amber cut in, sharing a look with Troy.

"Yes, you have, dear."

"I came because the first book you wanted to discuss sounded interesting. *The Second Coming*, by John Niven. It was such a fun read. Deep, as well." Emilia had a happy smile on her lips.

"I came because I was curious." Amber picked some crumbs from her lap. "And bored." She furrowed her brows. "And because my feet had simply carried me here without me even realizing it."

"We joined because you were discussing Jane Austen." Troy and Declan nodded at each other.

"You're my mate, so it's only natural I participate, *mo grah thu*."

"And I came because of Dre and *The Witcher* and stayed because of Jon." Barion kissed his mate.

"I still don't get it. You're saying it's not normal, you being friends — yet here you are. If it's so strange, then *why* are you here?" Sammy was obviously trying hard to understand.

Alerion looked at the witches who both shrugged, leaving the talking to him. "I think, son, it's because of the change Emilia mentioned. It was long overdue, and it had to come from the leaders. By leaving their respective people to be independent, they made the first step. The second was meeting you, becoming a part of the book club. By building new friendships with other powerful beings who are technically sworn enemies, all of them broadened their horizons. And because you are so adorable, Sammy, you became the glue keeping them together, even when they might have thought about quitting. Am I right?" Alerion looked around.

His mates, the witches, Emilia, Jon and Amber nodded. "In the beginning, I was torn between strangling these two"—Emilia pointed with her chin toward Declan and Troy—"or leaving. I did neither because I knew it would make you sad."

"Same here." Amber nodded wildly. "Even when I contemplated the wisdom of being in the same town as the others, I always knew I couldn't leave you."

"Our wolves decided to protect you the moment you offered us the first divine latte." Declan and Troy grinned.

"You let me stay in my cellar but never forgot me. It was just the thing I needed back then." Jon snuggled deeper into Barion's embrace.

"You see, son," Alerion started, "they came here of their own accord, but they stayed because of you. And they learned, and now they are changing the world. Even *I'm* changing, and I'm a later addition." He winked.

"I still think you'd have gotten along just fine without me." Sammy lifted a hand when they all opened their mouths to speak. "But I'm glad you gravitated to me, because you've become the family I thought I had lost. I'm grateful."

A lot of sniffling and hugging followed these words, confirming Alerion's suspicion that this group of people was meant to be together.

# Chapter Twenty

They were back in their apartment, Mr. Fluffy Sparkle Pants was fed and they were all showered. Declan looked at Troy, who nodded before he opened his cell, did some quick typing and the first chords of a tango filled the room. Alerion came in from the kitchen, where he had put the dishwasher on. His smile when he heard the music was like the sun rising in a cloudy sky.

"Oh, what is this?" He started swaying to the music, already perfectly in sync with the rhythm.

Declan grinned. "It's our not-very-subtle attempt to get to see more of your dance moves, beloved mate."

"Oh, I can give you all the moves you want." Alerion spun gracefully, coming to a halt directly in front of them. He first grabbed Troy, took him in a close embrace, twirled with him around the bed, turned around at the wall and brought him back to do the same with Declan, all the time floating to the music.

It felt heavenly, being led around the narrow space with such confidence. Declan's wolf was wagging his tail like crazy in his mind. Once both Declan and Troy were standing next to the bed again, Alerion gave them a show, his huge, muscular body giving new meaning to the temptation tango was famous for. While he was dancing, Alerion lost his clothing, piece by piece, and did the same with them, making it part of his performance to get all of them naked.

Declan didn't have to look at Troy to know his mate was as excited as he was. Both their cocks stood to attention, honoring the dance their mate was showing them.

The music changed, and the tango was replaced by something slow and sensual. Alerion's body was now gyrating with the smoothness of a snake, and his scales came out to heighten that image. Declan couldn't take his eyes from their gorgeous demon mate. Next to him, he heard Troy's breathing getting raspy.

Alerion came up to them, kissed first Declan, then Troy before he pushed both of them onto the bed. They lay there, Declan finding Troy's hand while their demon was looming over them, his upper body still moving gracefully, the image of a snake about to strike so vivid that Declan's wolf wanted to bare his neck in submission. It was a heady rush, knowing this powerful creature belonged to them, was theirs as they were his. Declan's cock jerked, pre-cum leaking down in a steady stream, dripping over his balls.

He could sense Troy wasn't faring any better. They both were ensnared by their mate's sensuality, the pure sexiness he was radiating. Alerion stroked their bellies, his claws just far enough out to add a little zing of danger to his ministrations, which had Declan's wolf panting with want. This was it. The thrill of being at the mercy of their mate, who could as easily eviscerate them as he could make sweet love to them. It was this dichotomy that revved Declan's lust up a to a thousand. Danger and love, wrapped in one appealing package.

Alerion had reached their groins, the claws making thin nicks along their hip bones, drawing just enough blood to perfume the air with a hint of copper. Declan moaned, gripping Troy's hand tighter. He could feel his wolf mate's arousal, scent it in the air, which made him even hornier, ready to do whatever Alerion had planned.

"You two are so magnificent. I don't know what I did to deserve you." Alerion bent down to kiss Declan's twitching, leaking cock, then did the same with Troy's and came up with his lips glistening with pre-cum. It was the most erotic thing, and if he ever had to masturbate again — the chances were slim with two eager mates, but still — this would be the perfect image.

"Want to take you both." Alerion sounded breathless, eager. *Perfect.*

"How?" Troy was squirming next to Declan, opening his legs, his thigh rubbing against Declan's, the skin contact making him hotter.

Alerion seemed to contemplate for a moment. They were still getting used to being a throuple and always happy to try new positions. "Troy, scoot back and lean against the headboard."

Troy let go of Declan's hand and wiggled backward on the bed until he was in position.

"Good boy," Alerion crooned. They had quickly found out that their wolves *loved* being good boys for their demon. Anybody else who dared call them that would have been confronted with the full wrath of two uber alphas. Alerion just got franticly wagging tails, figuratively speaking.

"Declan, go back between Troy's legs. Your back to his belly."

Declan thought he knew what their mate was planning and couldn't move fast enough. He pressed himself against Troy's broad chest, the skin-on-skin contact making him moan in happy anticipation.

Troy, too, seemed to have caught on, because he bent slightly forward, grabbed Declan's knees and lifted them up, exposing Declan's hole to their mate's hungry gaze. It was a rush like none other, being so defenseless in the presence of a superior hunter, who he knew would devour him. Declan couldn't wait.

He whimpered when Alerion crouched on the bed, the mattress dipping from his weight. He smiled, licking his lips with his demon tongue, which was longer and more flexible than anything Declan had ever felt. And that magic tongue was now dipping into his crack, licking along his taint, circling his already-twitching hole.

Declan snuggled up to Troy, his head rubbing on his mate's pecs, sending little sparks of pleasure through his body from the point of contact. Alerion seemed to be intent on torturing him, licking his groin, making little trips to his balls, the base of his cock, back to his taint. When he finally entered Declan's hole, he screamed in relief. Troy was still holding his legs, his fingers digging deep into his flesh, making everything sharper, better.

Alerion's talented tongue was stabbing inside his hole, coating his insides with spit, massaging his tight channel. The room was filled with groans and high-pitched pleas, but Declan wasn't ashamed once he realized he was making them. Anybody who got the same treatment and could stay still was a marble statue.

His incoherent noises seemed to spur Alerion on, because he started twisting his tongue inside Declan's hole, making him buck up in pure pleasure as far as Troy's hold would allow. His cock was bouncing on his belly, making obscene smacking noises every time Alerion dug deeper into him. If his mate went on like that, Declan would come from his tongue alone.

Sensing through the mate bond how close he was, Alerion drew back, his broad, satisfied grin smeared with spittle and pre-cum. He entered Declan's hole with two of his fingers, testing how stretched he already was. Thanks to their daily encounters in bed and on every surface that was sturdy enough, Declan knew his hole would give easily. Still, being the loving, perfect mate he was, Alerion found the lube in the bedside drawer and put some on his own cock before smearing the rest around Declan's hole.

"You've got him?" The question was for Troy, who panted next to Declan's ear.

"Yeah, yeah."

Troy's erection was like a branding iron at Declan's back, reminding him of another thing they still had to try — double penetration. The thought alone sent a violent shudder through his body.

"Not today, love." Troy's words were like a silken promise in his ears. They had talked about it and had agreed to try it when they knew they had an entire weekend off. These things took time and care.

"But we will." Alerion lined his cock up with Declan's hole, his crown nudging the entrance. Declan felt it opening, inviting their mate in.

With one long, swift move, Alerion buried himself to the hilt, his groan sending a breeze of warm air over Declan's chest and face. Behind him, Troy whimpered, his fingers kneading the flesh of Declan's thighs, his hot cock poking Declan's lower back, smearing it with pre-cum.

For a moment, they all held perfectly still. Alerion was looking at them, their position allowing him to see them both without having to turn his head.

"I love you both so much." Alerion bent forward, kissed first Troy, then Declan on the mouth.

"We love you, too." They said it in unison, the full weight of their feelings in those four words.

With a groan, Alerion straightened, pulling his cock out a few inches before ramming back in. The power of the thrust sent Declan's lower back crashing against Troy's cock, trapping it even further between their bodies. Troy moaned in pure pleasure.

Alerion started a rhythm that had nothing to do with the song playing in the background but was all his own. Declan whimpered, balling the sheets in his fists while Troy was grinding his groin against his back with every thrust their mate made. It seemed to go on forever, the wave building and building like it knew no end. Every time Declan thought they would finally reach the crest, Alerion managed to change his angle to send all three of them even higher. It was both the simplest and most complicated mating dance, synchronizing three partners on their way to absolute pleasure.

Declan reveled in every second, relishing the feeling of melting into both his mates, becoming one with them. Alerion started pumping faster, his grunts coming out almost pained. Troy was panting in Declan's ear, the staccato telling him his wolf mate was close as well. Declan felt the tingling start at the base of his nape, rushing down his back and expanding into his body like a drop of ink in water. He gasped, arching up his back at Alerion's next thrust, his cock and balls becoming impossibly hard, before he exploded like a geyser.

The wave had finally crested and was now crashing down on the shore, taking everything with it, grabbing his mates and dragging them under, the scent of their combined semen the olfactory proof of the heat Declan felt coating his back and ass and his insides.

It was utter bliss, being connected to both his mates, their cum and sweat mixing on their skin and the bedding — which they would have to change before going to sleep, thank you very much — making their fluids as one, as their minds and bodies were. As figures of speech went, this left a lot to be desired, but then again, Declan was caught in post-coital bliss and thinking was not high on his list of things to do.

Grinding against Troy to elicit further whimpering was — as was clenching his hole to give Alerion's cock a well-deserved massage. Both his mates grabbed him hard, bringing their bodies as close together as possible without actually becoming one person.

Troy sighed happily. "That was amazing. I can't wait for my turn."

His cock was already hardening against Declan's back, which in turn made Declan's shaft interested. Not to be outdone, Alerion's followed suit immediately.

They were in for a long night.

Declan couldn't wait.

# Epilogue

*A few months later*

"No, Tino, don't you worry. You were absolutely right sending that asshole packing. It will hopefully send a message to all the other idiots out there who think they can take advantage of you just because you're omegas. You're the ones in charge, and I'm afraid to say it'll probably take a few more firings until people get the message." Troy listened to the call Declan was having with their representatives.

Tino and Jules had fully taken over the running of the council now that they had their degrees, and things were going well, most of the time. Once a week, they had a short video call to fill Troy and Declan in on what was happening. If something major occurred, like an alpha asshole thinking he could run roughshod over people, they called in outside their scheduled times.

Announcing two omegas as the new council leaders had proven to be a genius idea. After the initial shock, many shifters expressed their support for this decision, showing that the time had been ripe to implement changes. Of course, there were always some who clung to the old ways, though their voices were drowned out by the cheers of the rest.

They hadn't heard from Fenris or the former council members, which they counted as a clear win. Fenris was probably licking his imaginary wounds somewhere in a realm hopefully far, far away, and the ex-council members were too busy trying to regain some of their money and dodging the effects of Mavis' and Maribel's spells to make trouble. If Troy and Declan had anything to say, it would stay that way.

The launch of *Demon Wars* had been an absolute success. People loved the game and were full of praise for the programming, as well as for the fun little videos Barion and Jon now released every month depicting different battles from the game. The two were already working on the sequel.

The demons were fully engaged in doing the videos, and because they were so well-behaved, Alerion had allowed Allienna to continue with their renaissance fair shows, which were a huge hit and additional advertising for the game and the videos.

At the moment, Barion and Jon were busy establishing another channel where people could watch the videos, interact with the demons via the platform and upload their own videos. The money they made with their videos went to several charities, because the demons didn't really need the money and were happy to be part of the whole thing. Alerion's relationship with his subjects had greatly improved, which in turn meant less stress for him, which led to a lot more sex for all three of them. Troy always liked it when things worked out perfectly.

"Yes. We'll talk at the end of the week. Have a great day, Tino, Jules. Bye." Declan pocketed his cell while they approached the door to Sammy's book shop. Their morning had been busy so far, and they needed some caffeine before they were able to face the rest of their itinerary for that day.

The wind chimes greeted them with their soft melody when they entered the shop but were drowned out almost immediately by the faint sobbing coming from the back of the store where the books that had yet to be listed were kept.

"Sammy?" Troy looked around the empty store. It was only twelve o'clock, which meant the teenagers who came to the store regularly weren't there yet, while the housewives and househusbands were back home to cook lunch. The sobbing went on.

Troy looked at Declan, who pointed to the back of the shop. Since nobody seemed to be here, they had no choice. Following the sound, they entered the small room that was stacked to the ceiling with crates and cartons full of books. In the small space left in the middle, an old table stood stacked high with even more books, and on that table, on a chair so old that Declan wondered why it was still functional — one of Sammy's pity-purchases, no doubt — sat Milo, his head in his hands, his shoulders shaking.

"Milo! What's the matter? Is everything all right?" Declan stepped forward, and Troy followed. There was no way they both could stand next to each other in that cramped space.

Milo's head came up abruptly and his red-rimmed eyes widened.

"Sorry. I'm sorry. Do you want your lattes? Sammy isn't here. Dre took him out for lunch."

"What we want, Milo, is for you to tell us what's going on." Troy put as much uber alpha dominance into his voice as he dared, hoping to make the young man finally confess his troubles and accept help. Milo grimaced.

"Milo." Declan added his own pinch of uber alpha when it became clear that the young man was thinking about being stubborn.

That one word seemed to be the straw that broke the camel's back. Milo's lower lip started quivering again and big fat tears streamed down his cheeks.

"M-my mom has her surgery tomorrow, and they say it's all going to be okay, but I don't know. I'm still so worried, and I think I'm going to flunk all my tests because I just can't seem to concentrate lately. And I think I'm in love with Quirion, but he doesn't even look at me, and I don't know what to do!"

Declan turned his head to throw a quick glance at Troy before he stepped forward to take Milo in an awkward hug across the table, trying not to bring down any of the book piles mounted around them. "Shh, it's fine. We're here for you. Your mom is going to be fine, I'm sure, and you're a genius. You'll nail those tests, and Quirion? Well, you'll have to talk to Sammy and Dre about him."

As if Declan's touch had broken a dam, Milo started sobbing violently, his entire body shaking from the force of his heaving. Apparently, he hadn't heard a word Declan had said.

Troy opened his mouth to add his own piece of advice while patting the front pocket of his slacks for his cell, because this was a situation where they needed back-up ASAP, when the hair on his nape stood up, sensing danger at his back. He swirled around, ready to fight whoever thought sneaking up on a werewolf was a good idea and came face to face with a green demon who was easily as tall as Alerion. The demon's fangs and claws were out, his scales rippling quickly over his body, his wings tucked in, probably because it was so damn narrow in the hall leading to this room. His eyes were glowing red, indicating he was highly agitated.

"Who hasch made Milo cry?"

Milo looked up from where he was still huddled over the table, Declan patting his back in an attempt to offer comfort.

"Quirion?"

Want to see more like this?
Here's a taster for you to enjoy!

# Bound to the Spirits:
# Laid to Rest
## T. Strange

### *Excerpt*

"Where do you want this box?" Morgan asked.

"Um, anywhere over there is fine." Harlan gestured vaguely in the direction of the kitchen. He had no idea what was in the particular box they were holding, but he was feeling too flustered to check. He knew his 'system' — or, rather, complete *lack* of one — would bite him on the ass later when he was actually trying to unpack and organize, but putting it off felt better than dealing with it at the moment.

"You know you don't have to help with this part, right?" he told them. "Moving *my* stuff, not the business stuff? I mean, you didn't really have to help with that, either. It's not part of your job description —"

"Please. The 'business stuff' was like three boxes. And I write my own damn job description — unless you've come up with a written statement of what my duties entail?"

Wide-eyed, Harlan shook his head.

"Yeah, I didn't think so," they laughed, setting the box down on a pile.

Charles swooped in and glanced at it. "Mm-m, that's a bathroom one."

Morgan frowned at him.

"I'll take it," he assured them.

Harlan sighed. Of course Charles could keep track of everything.

Harlan knew it was stupid to move his business out of his apartment—all three boxes of it, as Morgan had just pointed out—immediately followed by moving in with Charles. But that was how the timing had worked out with renting an office and Charles' lease on his old apartment running out. Technically there was no hurry on his end—Harlan's apartment was his as long as he wanted it—but it had seemed silly for Charles to move all his things and get them all unpacked, only for Harlan to dump a fresh pile of boxes on some nebulous future date. Not that Harlan had that many personal possessions... At least he'd *thought* he didn't, but there had been a surprising amount to pack up and load into the truck Charles had borrowed from a friend.

"Hey, does that mean I didn't have to help, either?" Hamilton—now Harlan's business partner at Laid to Rest Investigations—laughed.

*Shit.* Harlan swallowed hard. "Of course not. I'm sorry—"

"Hey." Hamilton clapped him on the shoulder. "Sorry... I was just kidding. I'm happy to help you two out. Matthew would have been here, too, but he had to work." He hurried back outside, probably to grab more boxes.

"Are you okay?" Charles asked, setting down the plastic tote he was holding.

Harlan noticed that Morgan was also giving him a concerned look. "Yeah. Sorry. I'm fine. It's just—a lot."

Charles nodded, giving Harlan a quick hug. "I know. But the end is in sight!" He turned in a slow circle, taking in the boxes covering every horizontal surface. "Well, the end of *moving*. Then it'll just be unpacking – and we can go at our own pace."

*Yeah. As long as we don't want to sit on the couch or find anything,* Harlan thought.

He just nodded at Charles, doing his best to smile.

"I think it's just a few more, then we can go for beer and pizza."

Harlan nodded again. He turned to leave the apartment to at least get some air and pretend to be useful by carrying something back inside, but his path was blocked by Hamilton, who was carrying a stack of boxes.

"Did I hear beer and pizza?"

"You did," Charles agreed. "As soon as the truck is empty."

Hamilton set the stack haphazardly by the door. "Then it's beer and pizza o'clock. These are the last boxes."

Charles whooped, grinning at the room. "Good work, team! I thought it would take us at least a few more hours."

Morgan snorted. "It would have gone a lot more quickly if you didn't have *so many* BDSM toys."

"Ha. Just be glad Harlan hasn't really started collecting his own yet or there'd be twice as many."

Harlan found that difficult to imagine. Charles already had one of every kind of whip, flogger, paddle and cane imaginable – if not multiples.

Charles mimed dusting his hands together. "All right, if that's it, let's get out of here. Why don't you just take one car?"

Harlan's stomach sank. He was already feeling really peopled out — which was sad, because these were the people he was closest to in the world — and there would only be *more* people at the restaurant. He'd been looking forward to at least driving over with just Charles.

"You guys go ahead. I'm gonna drop the truck off. Phil can give me a ride, and I'll meet you there. Harlan, you can order for me, okay?" Charles gave his shoulder a gentle squeeze.

*Great.* Now he wouldn't even have Charles in the car with him? And he would have to order not only for himself but also for Charles as well? Usually, it was the other way around. It made him feel like an immature jerk and a hot mess, but their system worked for them.

"Don't worry." Charles leaned over to kiss his cheek. "I wrote my order down for you."

*Well, that's something, anyway.*

Charles did that magical thing Harlan still couldn't figure out how to do that sent something directly from his phone to Harlan's.

"We can take my car," Morgan offered. "Hamilton's smells like thirty-year-old Tim Hortons."

Harlan wrinkled his nose. They weren't wrong.

Hamilton laughed. "Hey, I've spilled lots of *other* kinds of coffee in there! I don't think the stuff at the precinct is even 'no name'. It's...somehow even sketchier than that. It's probably not even real coffee."

"Yeah, you probably shouldn't be drinking that." Morgan shook their head, laughing.

Harlan found himself swept out the door and into Morgan's car. He barely had a chance to wave goodbye to Charles before he was gone.

* * * *

Morgan and Hamilton put in their beer and pizza orders almost as soon as they sat down at the restaurant, leaving Harlan frantically flipping through the menu. He chose the first thing that sounded edible and didn't have too many weird specialty ingredients. He ordered Charles' pizza, and he was about to tell the waiter what beer Charles wanted, but Hamilton shook his head.

"Nah, wait till he gets here so it'll still be cold."

Harlan nodded, feeling his cheeks flush a little. He was relieved when their drinks came. It meant that he had something to do with his hands, and he didn't have to talk.

He'd ordered Pepsi. He didn't drink alcohol — or only rarely. It tended to mess up his mood the next day.

He downed his first drink quickly and accepted a refill when the waiter came around again. Having that much caffeine so late in the day would probably fuck with his sleep, but he didn't want to switch to Sprite or something else. With a dark-coloured drink, he could at least pretend he was drinking beer like the others.

For the most part, Morgan and Hamilton were happy just talking to each other and leaving Harlan alone, which Harlan appreciated. Even knowing that they *knew* him and wouldn't expect him to carry the conversation, he still worked himself up sometimes.

He slowly relaxed. Luckily their booth was in a quiet corner, away from other groups, so he didn't feel *completely* overwhelmed.

The pizza arrived before Charles did. Harlan wondered if they should wait for him, but the other two started eating right away. Of course, they'd been helping move boxes for hours, whereas Harlan felt like he'd just sort of drifted around getting in the way.

He was starting to worry that Charles' food would get cold when Charles slid into the booth beside him, giving him a quick peck on the cheek before grabbing a slice and inhaling it.

Of course Charles' mouth was full when the waiter came around for his drink order.

Harlan fumbled in his pocket for his phone, which he'd put away because he knew it was rude to have it out while socializing. Though, again, he didn't think Hamilton and Morgan would really care.

Hamilton waved a hand at him. "It's okay. I've got this." He ordered for Charles, glancing at him for confirmation.

Harlan wasn't sure if it was even the right thing, but he gave up trying to get his phone.

Charles nodded, his lips slightly parted as he tried to swallow the too-hot sauce and cheese.

Harlan groaned inwardly. Hamilton could remember what his boyfriend liked to drink, and he couldn't?

Everyone else wolfed down their food while Harlan picked at his pizza and drank soda after soda.

"Oof, I'm stuffed." Charles leaned back with a groan, his hands folded on his stomach. Making sure Harlan was looking at him, he cocked his head in the direction of the door—his silent way of asking if Harlan wanted to leave.

Harlan nodded, moving his head as little as possible and hoping the others wouldn't pick up on their little exchange. That would have felt rude. He appreciated that Charles had come up with this little system for them. Again, he was pretty sure Hamilton and Morgan wouldn't actually mind, but this way he didn't have to say it himself. And he really did want to go home. Well, back to the box-choked apartment. *Ugh.*

At least he didn't have to work the next day. Laid to Rest didn't have any open cases, which was great for having time to move and unpack but not so great for his wallet or peace of mind.

*What was I thinking, trying to start my own business?*

\* \* \* \*

"Knock knock!" Benjamin Xun, one of the two remaining Toronto police mediums, stepped into the tiny Laid to Rest office, his hand raised as though he were about to knock. The door was open. The office got really hot and stuffy with both Harlan and Hamilton inside, and the solitary window didn't open.

Hamilton grinned at him. "Hey, Benjamin. It's been a while." Benjamin had visited them when they had first opened a few weeks earlier, but they hadn't seen him since—though Harlan had called him once for advice about dealing with a ghost. No. Not 'dealing with'. That wasn't what Laid to Rest was about. *Helping* a ghost. "Oh, *please* tell me you have a case for us."

Harlan leaned forward. He was glad Hamilton had said it, because he'd sure as fuck been thinking it.

Benjamin shook his head. "No, sorry, guys. I just wanted to drop off some 'congratulations on starting your new business' presents. I know it's a little late, but they were on back-order and… Anyway…here." He set four gift bags down on Hamilton's desk, which was closest to the door. "They're for you two, Morgan and Charles. Charles told me what kind of phones you all have." He cleared his throat, looking away from Harlan. "They're, uh, from Beth, too, but she wasn't sure if you'd want to see her."

She was right, but Harlan didn't say it out loud. "You'll have to, um, thank her for us."

Hamilton pounced on the pile of presents and started rooting around in one of them. He frowned as he held up its contents. "Oh, great. A weird-looking phone case and a flashlight. Thanks."

Harlan got up to take a closer look. "Really? Thank you!" He picked up the bag with his name on it and held it against his chest.

Hamilton snorted. "Jeez, kid, if I'd known you were that hard-up for a phone case, I would've gotten you one."

Harlan shook his head. "No, these are special."

Nodding, Benjamin pulled out his phone, which was already in a similar case. "The mesh on the back keeps ghosts from draining the battery, and" — he plucked the package out of Hamilton's hands — "it also comes with a warded screen protector so they can't get in that way, either. The flashlight is protected by the same mesh."

Hamilton whistled, leaning back in his chair with his hands laced behind his head. "Wow. Those must've cost you a pretty penny."

Harlan gulped. He hadn't realized that a warded screen protector was part of the case. Warding was expensive. "You really shouldn't have." He put the bag back on Hamilton's desk.

"Hey, don't worry about it. I was there when you learned how much it sucks for a ghost to drain your phone and light. I — *we're* — happy to help."

"Thank you so much." Realizing he should probably say something more and that he actually knew very little about Benjamin outside of their shared mediumship work, Harlan asked, "How are things going for you two?"

Benjamin let out a soft huff of laughter. "Well, I won't lie. It has been busy without you and Leo." Leo had been the Toronto Police Service's fourth medium until she'd lost her abilities six months earlier. "But we're managing." He smiled at Harlan. "It *has* helped that you guys are handling the less serious cases and we can just concentrate on murders."

Harlan shuddered. He definitely did *not* miss that part of being a police medium. Most of the ghosts he'd dealt with through Laid to Rest had died of natural causes or accidents. They tended to look more intact than murder victims, even if their deaths had been fairly gruesome.

"Anyway" — Benjamin patted the top of a gift bag with one hand — "I'll let you get back to it. Keep up the good work!"

Harlan and Hamilton glanced at each other. Harlan could see that Hamilton's computer screen only had a game of Solitaire on it. Harlan had been looking at Tumblr before Benjamin had come in.

"Thanks, we will!" Hamilton assured him, already trying to work open the plastic clamshell package on his new phone case.

"Say...say hi to Beth from us," Harlan added. He wasn't sure that he really meant it, but it seemed like the polite thing to do.

"I will." Benjamin waved at them and left.

"You're going to cut your finger off!" Harlan laughed, watching Hamilton saw at the packaging with his pocketknife.

"Mm-m, that sounds like someone who doesn't want his new flashlight and phone case," Hamilton said airily. "Besides, I'm just the muscle. I don't need all my fingers. In *fact*, I'm probably scarier *without* all my fingers!" He held up his left hand, his ring finger tucked against his palm so Harlan couldn't see it and wiggled his others.

"Yes, very scary." Harlan rolled his eyes. "You won't be able to marry Matthew without that particular finger, though," he pointed out.

"Oh, true." Hamilton let his finger pop up again. "I'll just have to make sure to cut off a different one, then."

Hamilton and his boyfriend weren't officially engaged yet, but Hamilton had confessed that he thought it was going to happen soon.

"And you're more than just the muscle," Harlan assured him, even though he knew Hamilton wasn't completely wrong. Hamilton had lost his small mediumship ability at the same time Leo had.

Harlan cleared his throat and quickly changed the subject. "We should have some scissors around here somewhere... Maybe..." Harlan went back to his own desk and dug through the drawers. "I don't. Do you?" *Great.* Another thing he'd have to buy for the business.

"Don't need 'em," Hamilton said without looking up from tearing the package open. He pulled out his phone, transferred it to the new case and applied the screen protector, which was completely transparent. Once they'd been painted, warding runes were invisible unless a medium was looking for them. "Eh. Not the most stylish thing, is it? Does this actually work?"

Harlan nodded. "They kept Benjamin and Beth's phones from getting drained when mine did, and their flashlights still performed."

Hamilton wrinkled his nose, tossing his phone down on his desk and beginning to attack the flashlight's package. "Well, hopefully we won't ever have to put that to the test."

"Agreed." Since it was unlikely that a rampaging ghost would appear in the office, Harlan decided he'd open his with Charles when he got home.

He and Hamilton had debated having the tiny office ghost warded but decided against it—in large part because of the cost, but also because they wanted *friendly* spirits to be able to come in. That was one of the main reasons they'd started Laid to Rest, after all. Harlan—and Hamilton and Morgan—wanted to work *with* ghosts as much as possible, rather than seeing them as a nuisance to the living and just getting rid of them.

Of course, it was unlikely that a ghost of any kind would show up. Most spirits were bound to the place they'd died, where they'd been buried or somewhere that had been important to them in life. Once they began haunting a place, it was very difficult for them to leave it.

Hamilton took out his new flashlight, loaded the batteries and clicked it on and off a few times...then a few more.

He groaned. "Would you mind if I take off early?"

Harlan shook his head. "No. I'm sure I can handle—"

"Don't say that! You'll jinx it!"

"I don't think anyone's coming in today. Better?"

Hamilton nodded.

"Besides, I told you that you don't have to be here at your desk all day. I can just call you if—*when*—I need you."

"Nope. This old workhorse needs to be in harness." He rapped the desk with both hands in fists, presumably as hooves. "Besides...Matthew's at work all day, and otherwise I'd just be kicking around the condo by myself."

"Oh, yeahhhh. Because sitting around *here* with me all day in an empty office is *so* much less sad!" Harlan teased him.

"Shut up. It is. I'm leaving now, but that doesn't change what I just said."

"Uh-huh. Say hi to Matthew for me."

"Will do. You say hi to Charles for me."

Harlan nodded and waved Hamilton out of the office.

He sighed, seriously considering following Hamilton out the door. But where would he go except home, which was cluttered with all Charles' and his junk, and if he wanted to sit down or find anything, he'd have to unpack. He didn't want to do that.

Besides...he kinda wanted to be alone after spending the day with Hamilton and Benjamin's unexpected visit, and Charles would be there until he left for work, probably six at the earliest.

It wasn't that he didn't want to see Charles! He just wasn't used to having someone else around *all* the time, and he hadn't realized how much he'd gotten used to having his own space.

It was fine. He'd adjusted to living alone. But he'd adjusted to working with Hamilton every day too, so he'd adjust to living with Charles.

It was fine.

He looked at the clock on the wall. It had come with the office, but it made him feel more legit, somehow, so he'd kept it. It was only three-thirty, and they were officially open until five—later by appointment—but there hadn't been a single phone call or anything all day. A few other occupants of the office building had stopped by, curious about the new agency. Harlan made a mental note to return the plate that someone had brought them 'welcome' cookies on. Hopefully

Hamilton would remember who they'd said they were and where they worked.

He shook his head. *Return a plate.*

When had he become such an adult?

# About the Author

Xenia Melzer was born and raised in a small village in the South of Bavaria. As one of nature's true chocoholics, she's always in search of the perfect chocolate experience. So far, she's had about a dozen truly remarkable ones. Despite having been in close proximity to the mountains all her life, she has never understood why so many people think snow sports are fun. There are neither chocolate nor horses involved and it's cold by definition, so where's the sense? She does not like beer either and has never been to the Oktoberfest – no quality chocolate there.

Even though her mind is preoccupied with various stories most of the time, Xenia has managed to get through school and university with surprisingly good grades. Right after school she met her one true love who showed her that reality is capable of producing some truly amazing love stories itself.

While she was having her two children, she started writing down the most persistent stories in her head as a way of relieving mommy-related stress symptoms. As it turned out, the stress-relief has now become a source of the same, albeit a positive one.

When she's not writing, she translates the stories of other authors into German, enjoys riding and running, spending time with her kids, and dancing with her husband.

Xenia loves to hear from readers. You can find her contact information, website details and author profile page at https://www.pride-publishing.com

PUBLISHING

Sign up for our newsletter and find out about all our romance book releases, eBook sales and promotions, sneak peeks and FREE romance books!

www.ingramcontent.com/pod-product-compliance
Lightning Source LLC
Chambersburg PA
CBHW031912190626
46814CB00003BA/868